Who Do You Think You Are?

Printed by CreateSpace, an Amazon.com Company

Cover Design by Antoinette Long

Photography: "Heaven's Trail" by Thomas Zimmer

I dedicate this book to my biggest fan
and the most extraordinary man I know,
Andrew Long,
whom I'm proud to call my son.

PART ONE

Chapter One

Mike and Pat Bigelow had been driving for hours and were treading on their last nerves. Which was why, Pat reasoned, they had been sniping and barbing at each other like two winos in a dumpster.

"Don't know why you insisted on coming to your old man's funeral," Mike said. "Not like he's ever done anything for us."

Pat was too weary to defend herself or her father. Not that Mike would understand, even if she tried.

"I have to be there for Mom," she said instead.

Mike laughed bitterly. "Your mom never done that much for us either, what with me being between jobs right now and you not working. She hasn't even offered to help."

Pat hadn't told her mother that Mike had been fired once again, and she quickly steered away from that touchy subject. The kinetically charged air, barely contained to the car, was Mike's calling card to a fight.

"I'll be able to go back to work in a couple months," Pat sighed. "As soon as this baby is born." The doctor was concerned about her pregnancy. He said waitressing was too physically demanding and that she would have to take a leave of absence.

They were coming into the northeastern outskirts of Pittsburgh, Pennsylvania, having driven from their home outside of Cleveland, Ohio. Mike was focused on maneuvering the rush-hour-jammed streets.

Pat watched her young husband's contemplative scowl as he drove, more aware from this angle of his growing paunch, though conceding he was still ruggedly handsome. *With a rugged personality to match,* she thought. But then, that was what had attracted her to him; his "bad boy" persona was in such sharp contrast to her upbringing. Being with him felt like an exciting coaster ride rather than the dull merry-go-round her life had been before falling in love with him. *They were both so young*, she told herself when his jokes got a little raw or cut a little too sharply, *he'll grow out of it.*

"Oh look," Pat exclaimed, "they've built a Wal-Mart." Their little Ohio town didn't have one of these giant stores. "Maybe we can get some stuff for the baby while we're here."

"Yeah, well maybe your mom can shell out some of that money she's got squirreled away," Mike said. "Now that your old man's gone, she'll have plenty more to spend on you and the baby," he grumbled.

Pat kept her mouth shut. She knew where this fishing line was cast, but she refused to ask her mom for any more money. The last time her mom had bailed them out, she had made it perfectly clear just what she thought of her deadbeat husband and his inability to keep a job.

Besides, her parents didn't have the money Mike thought they did. Her mother was just very frugal in budgeting her father's humble paychecks.

"Here we are," Pat sighed, relieved with the knowledge that Mike would be in a much better mood once he had a couple of drinks in him.

Her family was busy getting ready for the guests who would be arriving after the funeral the next day. Pat was excited to see them; grateful, too, for the buffer they provided between her and her irritable husband. Mike was so much more amicable around them; almost like a different person, she thought wearily, listening to him telling her mom that he wouldn't have missed coming for the world.

A plethora of emotions was embodied in the hug she gave her mom. After she left home a year ago, slamming the door behind her, she had talked to her mom on the phone but she hadn't talked to her dad. Now she would never be able to take back the angry words they had last spoken to each other when, defying him, she left to marry Mike.

The twins, Mary and Peggy, exclaimed and awed over her belly, and her mom, seeing how peaked she looked, told her to go upstairs and rest from the trip while she finished making dinner.

"I hope we're not putting you out, Robert," Pat said to her older brother, who had given up his room for them. When Pat left home last year, her sister Peggy had quickly snatched up her bedroom, saying she needed her own space.

"Naw, I sleep on the couch most nights anyway," Robert said good-naturedly.

Even Mike's baiting comment as he dropped their bags in the bedroom, "Sure, leave me to fend for myself with your family," couldn't dampen the relief she felt in having a few minutes of tranquility.

Descending the stairs after her much-needed nap, she saw, as predicted, her husband was relaxed and bantering with her brother about their rival teams, the Cleveland Browns and the Pittsburgh Steelers.

"There are some wonderful smells coming from that kitchen," she said to her sister, Mary, who was setting silverware on the table for dinner.

"Mom's been cooking for two days, even though the neighbors keep bringing food," Mary said. We have enough here to open a soup kitchen!"

Going into the kitchen determined to help, Pat ached with mourning her father's absence, so acute in this house and in her mother's countenance.

As a family, they had never been very emotionally demonstrative, preferring to act out their feelings with deeds, like her mother was now doing with her excessive cooking. So when Pat came into the kitchen and gave her mother an impromptu hug, it surprised them both. Awkwardly, they separated, her mother saying, "Go wash your hands for dinner."

In the bathroom, Pat put her head in her hands and cried for her dad, who would never again be able to comfort her with his usual ministration, "Everything's gonna be all right, sweetie."

A sharp pain pierced her side, causing her to sit on the edge of the bathtub to steady herself. *Ssssh sweetie*, she told her belly, *everything's gonna be all right.*

"You look as white as a ghost," Peggy remarked as she came out of the bathroom and took her place at the dinner table. "Are you all right?"

"I'm fine," she lied. "The doctor thinks this baby is anxious to be born early is all."

"Your doctor is a quack," Mike said for the benefit of everyone at the table. Then, seeing their dumbfounded expressions, he defended himself. "He's got her on bed rest and won't let her do a goddamned thing. According to him, the world stops when a woman gets pregnant."

Her mother shot her a look of concern and Pat said, "I'm okay, Mom. Really."

Everyone was quiet, concentrating on eating and avoiding the empty chair at the head of the table.

Eventually, her mother said, "The funeral isn't until tomorrow afternoon, so you'll have plenty of time to rest up."

Changing the subject, Pat asked, "How's your job, Robert?"

All through college he had coveted a job at The Lexington Company, the largest medical machine research and manufacturing company in the eastern United States. He took the courses they recommended and kept them apprised of his academic progress. It was more or less expected they would hire him when he graduated, but he was over the moon when it happened.

"It's great, I love it," her brother said. "It sure is keeping me busy. We just launched a new machine that can look into your womb and watch the baby move around."

"That's amazing!" Pat said.

"It really is," he said. "Too bad it won't be finished before you have your baby."

"Speaking of babies," Peggy said, "my hairdresser told me the owner is having a blowout party for his new baby tomorrow and practically the whole town is invited."

"I don't know about the whole town," Robert said, "but he did invite all the employees." Directing a look to his mother, he added, "But there will be so many people there, they won't even miss me."

They lapsed into another uncomfortable silence, not wanting to bring up the subject of the funeral. Pat glanced at Mike, who was being unusually quiet.

He caught her eye and shot her back a look that said, *what?*

She smiled at him, remembering all the times he had been here for dinner while they were dating. She hadn't realized until tonight, now sitting around this old dining room table, what a lifetime ago that seemed.

The silence was broken again when Pat asked Mary about her boyfriend and both she and Peggy enthusiastically filled her in on all the details of their love lives and the homecoming dance that was coming up.

Robert and Mike excused themselves to go watch TV, and Pat's mom got up to clear the table. "Why you've hardly touched your food, honey," she said to Pat. "I'll put it in the refrigerator so you can eat it later."

Carrying some dirty plates and following her mother into the kitchen, she intended to ask the question that had been uppermost on her mind since her mom's phone call. She was desperate to know if her father was still angry at her when he died.

"Here, Mom, let me clean up the kitchen," Pat said as she ran water in the sink for the dishes.

"Nonsense," her mother said, covering Pat's plate of food with tin foil so it could be warmed up in the oven later. "It's best I keep busy."

"That's just like you, Mom," watching her deftly wrap the foil around her plate. "You're always worrying about us," Pat said. "Can't I worry a little about you?"

"There's enough worry to go around, I suppose," her mother said sadly.

"Did he. . ." Pat began, but was cut off by the girls bringing in more dishes from the table, arguing about what they were going to wear to the funeral tomorrow.

Pat didn't hear them suspend their dispute mid-sentence, stunned by the sight of her suddenly clutching her side and bending, as she stifled a groan and sank to the floor.

Her mom rushed to support her weight so she wouldn't fall, saying to Peggy, "Go get Mike."

Pat tried to stop her, "No, Mom, don't call Mike. I'm okay. I must just be over excited." She didn't want to tell her mom that she didn't have health insurance and she knew Mike wouldn't want to take her to the hospital.

But Peggy had already gone to fetch him and a minute later he ambled into the kitchen, annoyed by the interruption.

Her mom told him he should take Pat to the hospital, but Mike promptly dismissed her suggestion, saying, "She'll be all right, she just needs to rest." Turning on his heels, he walked back to the TV and the game he had been watching.

"I'll be all right, really," she said, forcing herself to stand. "I'm just tired is all. I think I'll go upstairs and lie down."

She was relieved the pain had subsided enough for her to make her way upstairs and retrieve her nightgown and toothbrush from her suitcase. Lying in bed, she listened to her mother arguing with Mike and was tempted to get up and go back downstairs, but she was just too tired.

She overheard Mike say, "She's my wife, I'll make the decisions for her!" The question of just whom she should defend crossed her mind; her mother or her husband?

Her brother's window was open and a gentle breeze was blowing the sheer white curtains into the room, creating a soothing lullaby, gently fanning away the fear, tension and grief. This is what home feels like, she thought dreamily as she drifted off to sleep.

Much later, she woke as she felt her husband fall into bed and begin to snore before his head had barely put a dent in the pillow.

She lay there listening to the night sounds of her old home. She heard the crickets outside and tried to pinpoint the moment she had gone from young, carefree "Patty" to "Pat," the adult, responsible one. Probably about the same time she had cut her hair from her fashionable flip to the short sensible hairstyle she now wore. *Somebody's got to be the adult*, she reasoned.

She had loved growing up in this house. What seemed like such a boring life at the time, now felt like safety and security. She remembered catching lightning bugs and showing her little sisters how they lit up in her hands, telling them to watch how the bones in her fingers were illuminated as if she had no skin.

She imagined Robert's new machine was like that, lighting up her womb and showing the baby inside her belly. *I wish I could see it*, she thought as she drifted back to sleep.

Chapter Two

Andrew Lexington was having a restless night, tossing in his bed like a ship that had lost its mooring in a storm. He wasn't prone to sleepless nights, nor to waves of worry. He felt a storm approaching, but try as he might, he couldn't place its source.

Later, he would look back on these moments of apprehension, chastising himself for not paying more attention to his foreboding.

Getting out of bed to let his wife sleep, he went into the nursery to check on his daughter, Georgia, and saw that she too was having a fitful sleep, whimpering and clutching at her bed covers.

"Papa's right here, sweetie," he said, picking her up and sitting with her in the old rocking chair his mother had used to calm him when he was a baby. Softly singing the same lullabies his mother had sung to him, he and Georgi rocked peacefully until the sun's rays began to peek through the curtains, bringing with them all the hope and promise of a new beginning.

"Let's get you bathed and pretty for your mama," he said, kissing her cheek to wake her. "Today is your christening day, sweet one. Rise and shine so I can show you off to the world."

He placed her in her plastic tub and chuckled as she blew bubbles at him. She looked like a little porcelain doll, he thought; small boned and delicate like her mother. Cleaning her up, he again saw the birth mark on her little derriere and told her the story of how her Auntie Mae believed the mark was put there by God Himself when His hand pressed the first breath of life into her little body.

Marie woke to the sound of her daughter's coos as Andrew wafted Georgi into their bedroom, clean and sweet-smelling; setting her ceremoniously down on the bed before he too climbed between the sheets to watch his daughter's anxious anticipation of her breakfast.

"Wake up, Mama," he exclaimed. "It's time for our daughter to eat and get ready for church." He looked at his wife and felt the familiar pull of his heartstrings. Her long blond hair fell in tangles over her slender shoulders and she gave him a sleepy smile.

When he first saw her eight years ago, standing with a group of girls across the hall of the Student Union, his immediate thought was that she was the perfect "Dove Girl" - one of those wholesome beauties on the popular soap commercial who radiated class and confidence. She was the type of girl that every other girl wanted to hate for her perfectly-formed features and long graceful legs, but couldn't dislike because she was so kind and unpresumptuous. Over the last eight years, her youthful beauty had bloomed into a lovely elegance. He said, "Sweetheart, you're more beautiful right now than the day I married you."

Marie smiled with a contentment only the truly loved can know, and as she arranged herself for Georgi's hungry mouth, she thought how lucky she was to have such a loving and kind-hearted husband. His virile good looks, golden curls and china-blue eyes had ensured him plenty of women in college to choose from, but he had loved her unabashedly since the moment they first met that fateful day in May of their junior year. Drew was lean and strong from his daily track team practices; but unlike a lot of the other jocks she had known, he had a sensitive and contemplative nature and would rather study or go to a movie than to a party.

The three of them lay in bed while Georgi suckled, as had become their custom since her birth, almost a month ago.

"I can't wait for the rest of the family to finally meet her," Marie sighed.

There was a quiet knock on the door and Mae came in with a tray of coffee.

"Y'all can't lay around here for long, you know; the caterers will be here any minute and you'll still be in your PJs," Mae said.

"Yes ma'am," Andrew respectfully retorted as he headed to the shower. He left Marie and Mae talking about last minute seating arrangements for dinner, calling over his shoulder to remember not to seat Aunt Emily and Aunt Ruth at the same table.

"Remember what happened at our wedding?" he reminded them.

"Nobody's going to forget that cat fight for a long time," Mae said. "Don't you worry, Andrew, we've got it under control."

Andrew smiled. Not many people talked to him with such license as Mae. His parents had hired her as their nanny-housekeeper when he was six years old and she had quickly become his second mother; even more so since his parents' untimely death in a car crash three years ago. She was short and stocky with a no-nonsense personality and he had quickly learned not to sass her! She had a heart of gold but could be as tough as his father when it came to discipline and had certainly made Andrew tow the line. Mae would not tolerate any "high falootin' shenanigans," as she put it, and he had grown up knowing that, except for the grace of God, he was no better than anyone else, even though he had a more comfortable and secure life than most of his friends.

He let the hot shower soothe him as he thought of his cantankerous aunts, Emily and Ruth. He wasn't anxious to hear what they would have to say to him today when they found out Mae and Joe would be Georgi's godparents. *I'm sure they'll give me a piece of their mind*, he thought.

It had been an easy decision for Andrew and Marie to choose Mae and her husband, Joe, as Georgi's godparents. But he knew that his aunts would strongly protest that decision for the single reason of their skin color. He had to laugh to himself at the irony of the two aunts being in agreement on anything. Still, he had to steel himself for the confrontation that he knew was coming.

He wondered briefly if that was the source of his previous apprehension; he didn't want his daughter exposed to all that bigotry and bitterness so early in her life. *Plenty of time for that later*, he thought.

Forcibly re-routing his thoughts, he focused instead on the family, friends and employees who would be at Georgi's debut. He hoped she would be the first of many more children, but he was prudently withholding his thoughts on that subject from Marie for the time being.

Marie had just finished making the bed when he appeared from the steam of the bathroom and she offered to pour him a cup of coffee.

"I'll get that, honey" he said, taking the carafe from her and pouring them both a cup. "Where's Georgi?"

"Mae took her down to the guest house to show her off to her parents." Mae's elderly parents had arrived late last night from Memphis and had not yet met Mae's newest "young'un." "Oh, and she said she made breakfast rolls and you should go get some before the caterers arrive and shoo you out of the kitchen."

A flurry of activity was already in progress when Andrew arrived downstairs: the tent company was setting up large event tents; the caterers were dressing the tables he and Joe had set up on the lawn the night before; and the flowers had just arrived.

Mae's affable husband, Joe, who prided himself on keeping the yard in immaculate condition, was directing traffic and dispersing directives to the workers. He loved being in charge and giving orders, as he was usually on the receiving end of Mae's.

Joe was never without his lovin'-life-grin, which was as much a part of his face as the evenly spaced freckles across his nose. He gave Andrew one of those slow grins now. "It's going to be a mighty fine day, Drew," he said in greeting.

Simultaneously, Andrew heard a familiar, but unexpected voice calling out, "Hey, Drew, I heard there was a party here today!"

"Judy!" Andrew ran to embrace his gregarious little sister, who usually had a sassy word on her tongue for him. Judy was the free spirit of the family, with a carefree attitude that belied the seriousness of her work at a women's shelter in Cleveland.

Andrew often marveled at the apparent contradiction between Judy's chosen career and her character. Knowing Judy as he did, he could easily assume she didn't know the meaning of the words "victim" or "abuse." She was far from a victim and would likely take down the person who was stupid enough to attempt to abuse her. He remembered, with a wince, their childhood spats - where more than once he had found himself in a headlock he couldn't wrestle out of. She was the most confident and self-assured person he knew.

She wasn't a beautiful girl, not like his Marie. As a child, she sported a gaggle of unruly auburn curls and a personality to match. She used to walk around in their mom's high heels with a crown on her head, declaring herself to be "the most high awesome one." Her personality and confidence made her a heroine in his eyes.

He also knew the depth of her sensitivity and compassion, evidenced by the love she showed "her girls." She didn't get home as often as he wished she would because of her dedication to them.

"I thought you said you couldn't get away from work?" Andrew said.

"I got someone to cover for me," Judy answered. "I couldn't miss my niece's big day! Where is she?"

As if on cue, Mae was jogging across the yard, bouncing Georgi on her ample hip, in order to embrace her other 'young'n,' the girl she had helped raise from a toddler.

Marie came out of the house just in time to greet Judy and to witness Ted and Denise's arrival. Mae's brother, Ted, and his very pregnant wife, were walking around the house from the driveway to a pandemonium of greetings, causing Joe to settle everyone with his declaration that it was time to get to the church.

Ted went to fetch his parents from the guesthouse and escort them into one of the cars that would take them all into town.

"Don't see why we couldn't get one of those fancy limos and ride in style," Joe bantered with his wife.

"Now don't you start, old man," Mae said. "Bad enough having those caterers crawling all over the place!"

Andrew and his wife exchanged a smile while Judy said, "Nice to see that nothing's changed around here. I swear, Joe, you just love to push her buttons and watch her go off."

Joe gave a satisfied smile in response.

~ ~ ~ ~

The church was crowed when they arrived, with their friends, some of Andrew's employees, and the usual Sunday church-goers. They squeezed in wherever there was room while Marie and Mae took Georgi to the dressing room.

A gasp escaped from one of the back pews when, later, they rose to ascend to the alter. Andrew knew it had to be one of his aunts and quickly looked to Mae to reassure her, but Mae's head was held proudly high.

The minister took Georgi in his arms and put his hand on her small head.

"The hand of God is on this little girl," he said, "who, growing strong through adversity, will become a testimony to God's strength and mercies."

With a shiver, Andrew recalled his nighttime fears, but they were immediately replaced with pride as the minister held Georgi up, saying, "I baptize you, Georgia Marie Lexington, in the name of the Father, the Son, and the Holy Ghost."

The small church rang with applause as they made their way out into the bright sun.

"Let's go home and eat," Joe said. "I've worked me up a mean appetite!"

~ ~ ~ ~

"I'm going to take Georgi upstairs and feed her so she'll be a more pleasant guest of honor," Marie said to Andrew when they arrived back at the house.

Andrew kissed both of their foreheads, "I'll entertain our guests in the meantime, sweetheart."

Stepping onto the back veranda, he had to marvel at what the caterers had done in just a few short hours. His lovely yard had been transformed into something magical. Far from obstructing the grace of the slow slope of lawn leading down to the mighty Monongahela River, the tents had given it a Gatsby-like appearance. The sunlight was reflecting off of them and the slow-moving river beyond, making an elegant backdrop of sparkling diamonds.

Judy came up behind him and let out a sigh as she wrapped her arms around his waist.

"Oh Drew, it's so beautiful. Don't you wish Mom and Dad were here to see this?"

Andrew turned and put his arm around her shoulders. "You're reading my thoughts, Sis. Every time I look at Georgi, I think about how much they wanted grandchildren, and now...."

Their private moment was abruptly interrupted when Aunts Emily and Ruth, with Ruth's husband, Bob, in tow, descended upon them.

"My goodness, Andrew," Ruth said, "What in the world were you thinking by letting *those* people be godparents to your daughter?"

"Your parents, God rest their souls, would roll over in their graves if they knew," Emily added.

"Why hello Aunties, Uncle Bob," Judy said, facetiously. "So nice to see you again."

Judy's sarcasm did little to deter them, although Emily leaned in and lowered her voice.

"How can you let those colored people raise your daughter?"

"What will people say?" Ruth, who had no intention of lowering her voice, snarled.

Judy exploded, "People will say that it's the parents' decision to make!"

They turned on her in tandem with fire in their eyes. "And you, Judy," Emily said, "how can you let him do this when you're the logical choice?"

"Oh no," Judy said. "I'm the least logical choice. I have no experience with children. Why, Mae and Joe practically raised us."

Andrew put an end to the dispute, saying, "We are in complete agreement on this. I'm sorry if you don't like it."

"Well!" Ruth said, pulling the still-silent Bob back toward their car. "You haven't heard the last from us about this."

"You're bringing a curse upon your family, Andrew," Emily called out as they rounded the corner of the garage in a hasty retreat.

"Oh!" Judy blustered. "Their narrow-minded, bigoted attitudes just infuriate me!"

"Still fighting all the injustice in the world, are you Sis?" Andrew smiled.

"What was all that about?" Mae's brother, Ted, who was approaching them from behind, asked.

Judy's answer was to stomp off across the yard, while Andrew said, "Oh, you know my aunts, mean-spirited as ever. I'm just glad that Marie wasn't here to witness that drama."

Nodding his head in agreement, Ted said, "Your wife is the most guileless person I've ever met and very sensitive, to be sure."

"She believes that everyone is good at heart," Andrew said. "It sets her in a tail-spin when she encounters people like that, she just can't understand it."

"Not that any of us can, really," Ted said. "What made them so mean, anyway?"

Andrew explained that his mother and her sisters had grown up on the threshold of poverty. "When my mom married my dad and his company started doing well, rather than being happy for their sister, they got jealous. Then my parents made the mistake of paying for Ruth's son's college education, thinking they were helping, but it just made things worse."

"No good deed goes unpunished," Ted sighed.

"Here's the party girl now," someone standing beside them said. Turning, Andrew watched as Marie descended the veranda steps with Georgi.

Marie was wearing a more elegant version of Georgi's christening gown and Andrew wished he could stop time and capture this moment forever. The pictures that the cameras around him were clicking off wouldn't do justice to the full smile that played on Marie's beautiful face, nor to the corona of sunlight surrounding them. She glowed with complete fulfillment.

His father-in-law's slap on the back spoke into his thoughts, "Our girls are a sight to behold, aren't they, Andrew?" he asked.

"They certainly are, Frank," Andrew said, shaking his hand. "It's good to see you."

He meant it. Frank was his rock. He had come to rely on his in-laws, Frank and Louise, in the three years since his parents' fatal car accident, when Andrew had to step into his father's shoes and run the family business. Frank always had good advice to give and his wife, Louise, was generous with her wisdom and encouragement.

Frank wore a perpetual crew cut, a remnant from his distinguished military career. A born leader himself, Frank felt no need to impose himself in Andrew and Marie's life, and Andrew appreciated Frank's quiet and constant availability to discuss any thoughts or problems Andrew might be grappling with. They had their difference of opinions, for sure, but Frank had a way of stating his own opinion while not devaluing Andrew's. He credited Frank for most of the major business decisions he'd made since taking over the leadership of his father's dream-child, The Lexington Company, or TLC, as they affectionately called it.

Frank's wife, Louise, interrupted their moment to announce that the photographer wanted some shots of the family.

"The dreaded pictures," Frank said. "The necessary evil of all great occasions. Come Andrew, let's record these beautiful ladies for posterity."

As the photographer was making endless arrangements of arms and heads, Judy asked Mae, "Does the minister usually prophesy over the babies he christens?"

"Only when he feels the calling. I just knew our baby girl had the hand of the Lord on her," Mae said proudly.

"Still," Judy said, "it was a little disconcerting hearing him say that Georgi will go through adversity." Judy knew all too well the kinds of adversity women suffered. She saw it every day at her clinic.

"Not to worry," Andrew said. "She's got her papa watching out for her."

"Smile now," the photographer said, snapping the picture.

After countless promises of 'just one more,' they were finally free of their pictorial duties and were able to mingle with their guests. *There must be over three hundred people here*, Andrew marveled. They had planned enough food and drink for everyone invited, although Andrew hadn't anticipated such a considerable response, and was warmed by it. He had given an open invitation to the employees of his company and most of them were here. Most everyone except Robert, and he reminded himself once again to call and offer his condolences on his father's passing.

This gala was long overdue for the employees of TLC. The last three years had been grueling on everyone. Henry Lexington, a pioneer in his field and the beloved helmsman of TLC, died suddenly in the prime of his life; coinciding with the apex of many years of hard work on their newest invention. There had been formidable pressure on everyone to make their deadlines without their leader and the inspiration behind it all. Extraneous to all that, the boss's twenty-nine year old son was taking over and attempting to fill his shoes.

At present, there were two camps of people at TLC: those who were impressed with Andrew's gumption and accomplishments thus far; and those who still thought of him as "the spoiled little rich kid." Thankfully, the first camp was much larger than the second.

The calypso band was softly playing a metallic melody, mingling perfectly with the laughter floating up from clusters of people gathered across the lawn.

Andrew did his best to talk to everyone for a few minutes, although with so many old friends and new employees, it was difficult keeping conversations short.

He occasionally gained possession of his daughter to show her off to his friends, but she was quickly snatched out of his arms by someone wanting to hold and admire her. He was glad to see that Marie had changed her into an outfit more comfortable and conducive to the man-handling she was getting. *Good thing she's so good-natured*, he thought.

His best friend and college roommate, who had morphed into his right hand man at TLC, was standing with a group of ladies by the dock. *Leave it to John*, he thought, smiling. The confirmed bachelor, with his smooth charm and quick wit, has once again managed to draw the single ladies to him as easily as a puppy summons a smile.

Andrew had met John freshman year, when Andrew had walked into his assigned dorm room that first day and found

John propped up on one of the beds, shoes and all, smoking a cigar.

"Hey, ya'll," John drawled through his Mississippi accent. His winsome insolence usually got him what he wanted, Andrew quickly learned. He also learned that John had his back. Always. They were polar opposites in many ways. John was a football jock and muscular. He was the embodiment of "tall, dark and handsome," with southern manners and charm to boot. He never joined a fraternity because he wanted to room with Andrew, but he went to most all of their parties. His football buddies were jealous of the bond the two of them shared and made fun of skinny, bookworm Andrew. They continually conspired to lure Andrew into traps they set to embarrass or humiliate him, but John sprung each one in turn.

"Hey, John!" he called out to him now as he walked toward the dock.

John extracted himself from his companions to meet up with Andrew. "Nice gig," he said. "Almost makes me want to get married and have kids myself."

Andrew laughed. Knowing John as well as he did, he truly doubted whether the thought of marriage spent more than mere seconds passing through his mind.

Andrew pulled the keys to the boat out of his pocket and tossed them in the air to John. "Joe was able to fix that intake problem we had the last time we were fishing, so you shouldn't have any trouble with it."

"Thanks, Drew. I'm sure the ladies would love a little cruise up the river."

"Oh, by the way," Andrew said, "do you know why those kids over by the bar are acting so hostile?" He was referring to a group of young TLC employees whom he felt were sneering at him. "I got a very caustic response when I tried to talk to them just now."

"The guy in the middle, Seth, the stocky one with the short blond hair, was a friend of the man in accounting we fired last week for embezzling," John said. "I think Seth was in on it, but we haven't been able to prove it yet."

"So why did they come?" Andrew asked. "They have a very obvious distaste for me."

"Probably more out of curiosity than anything else," John said. "I'm keeping an eye on them, although I'd feel a lot more comfortable if Robert were here. They seem to respect him."

"But not us," Andrew finished for him. "I just don't get why they feel entitled to steal from us or how they justify it. But we've already had this conversation and this isn't the day to discuss it again."

Dismissing the subject to be dealt with at another time, Andrew said, "Have fun on the boat with your cortege."

Looking for a little fun himself, he walked toward the table where Judy was sitting with family and some friends and realized too late that they were in the middle of the perpetual argument about Judy moving back home.

He had turned to walk away when Judy called out, "Come here, Drew, and tell them."

Reluctantly, he returned to the table and explained for what seemed like the umpteenth time, "I keep telling her that her room is here for her; full time, part time, whenever she wants it." Winking at Judy, he added, "She loves what she does and I'm sure the women she helps are grateful."

"Harrumph," Mae said, standing up from the table and taking a sleeping Georgi from Marie's lap. "Don't know why she can't do what she loves right here in Pittsburgh and leave Cleveland be."

Marie offered to take Georgi up to bed, but Mae waved her off. "Talk some sense into that other heart-o-mine, will you?"

Once Joe thought Mae was out of earshot, he said sympathetically, "Don't pay her any attention, Judy."

"You think you're whispering when you're talking loud as day, you deaf old man," Mae called over her shoulder as she climbed the steps to the veranda.

Their laughter twinkled with the lights strung up on the dock and the tents, which glistened brighter in the fading light.

A contented hush fell over the table as they watched people dance to the music of the steel drums.

"The mosquitoes are starting to get to me," Ted's wife, Denise, said a few minutes later. "I think I'll go inside and keep Mae company."

As she was leaving, Andrew suggested taking the party indoors, but nobody seemed to want to move. They sat in a contented hush, lulled by the retreating sun.

Denise's scream burst violently from the house, reverberating over the water like a struck bell.

Andrew was the first one inside and up the stairs, rushing toward the cries coming from the nursery. They became even more hysterical as realization seeped through the shock of seeing Mae's body sprawled out on the floor.

She met him in the hall wailing, "Georgi's gone!"

Chapter Three

John was motoring Andrew's boat back into the dock when he saw the flashing red lights echoing off the trees and roofline of the house. *What the hell?* he thought, quickly tying off the boat and making sure the ladies were on solid ground before sprinting up the lawn. Peripherally, he saw the remaining guests staring in stunned silence at the house, their knotted brows urging him faster up the stairs.

Mae was on a stretcher, being transported out the front door by EMTs when he entered. She appeared to be unconscious. Ted was assisting his pregnant wife out to another waiting ambulance. There were policemen everywhere. John looked frantically for Andrew, instead finding Frank in the living room talking to a detective. He barged into their conversation, asking, "What's going on?"

"Georgi's been kidnapped," Frank answered in brief, continuing to him and the detective what he knew of the events leading up to Denise's scream.

John listened in disbelief as Frank told them that Denise had found Mae laying on the floor of the nursery and Georgi was nowhere to be found.

"Where were you?" the detective asked John.

"I was out on the boat. Where's Andrew?"

"I'd like to get your statement if you don't mind," the detective said, ignoring John's question.

"Of course, but I have nothing to say that could help you. I've been out on Andrew's boat for the past couple of hours with some of the other guests."

After giving the detective the names of the girls he had been with on the boat, and being told not to leave the premises, John dashed up the back staircase to find Andrew, eyes red-rimmed, pacing the hall in front of his bedroom door, while the police blockaded the nursery and front staircase with yellow tape.

"I heard," John said as he grabbed Andrew in a bear hug and held on tight, trying to impart some life and strength into Andrew's seemingly bloodless body.

"Where's Marie?" he asked as he supported Andrew's slump to the floor, propping him up against the wall.

"She's in the bedroom with Judy and Louise. The paramedics are treating her for shock," Andrew said, barely audible.

Squatting down in front of Andrew, John said, "It looks like you could use something too."

Andrew's head shot up, but whatever life the suggestion had sparked in him, quickly died. He shook his head. "I need to be alert," he said.

Looking Andrew straight in the eye, John promised, "We'll get the bastard who did this."

"I just want my daughter back," was all Andrew could say before convulsing with deep sobs.

John held and rocked him, saying again and again that they would find Georgi.

John's blood was coursing through him like a mad river that had flooded its banks, tearing down everything in its path and sweeping with it all reason and logic, heaving with revenge and the need to destroy.

He was trying desperately to remember the world before it had shifted on its axis, trying to find sense in the nightmare they had been thrown into. It seemed days ago that he was catching the boat keys Andrew was tossing to him. He recalled their laughter and the sounds of the music as if they were distorted, like looking at an image in a funhouse mirror, almost grotesque in retrospect.

A sneering smile was teasing at his memory; laughing at him. Seth McPherson. That's who he and Andrew had been talking about when Andrew tossed him the keys. Suddenly Seth's face was full blown in John's mind and all he could see was his insolent, contemptuous, mocking sneer.

Seth's buddy, Bill, had been stealing from them for over a year before John had been able to prove it and have him arrested. John had been watching Seth closely for proof that he, too, had been stealing company funds, but hadn't been able to pin anything on him as yet.

Seth had a cocky demeanor that spoke of knowing things others didn't. John didn't trust him for a second. It hadn't occurred to him, until then, that Seth's vendetta against them, and Andrew in particular, could be something much more personal than taking money from TLC's bank account.

John realized that his own body was now shaking with rage, fusing with guilt at his own short-sightedness.

Frank came up the back stairs to tell them the detective would like to speak to them in the kitchen.

"John and I will talk to him if you want to stay with Marie," Frank said to Andrew.

"No," Andrew said, standing up. "They gave her a sedative and Judy and Louise are with her. I need to talk to him."

Detective Lester McGinty was waiting for them in the kitchen when they descended the back stairs. "I'd like to get a statement from you, Mr. Lexington," he said.

Detective McGinty was a beefy Irishman who looked like he could handle miscreants with one hand, while making the obligatory, but unnecessary, call for back-up with the other.

John cut to the chase and said, "I think I know who did it."

"Who?" they all chorused.

"Remember Seth McPherson's attitude at the party?" John asked Andrew. John turned to Frank and Detective McGinty and told them the story of his stealing friend, and how he also suspected McPherson of stealing from the company. John recounted Seth's mocking them at the party, and that he and Andrew had wondered why he had come, since McPherson's hatred of them was so obvious.

Andrew slumped into a chair at the table and the others followed suit and sat down.

"Was Seth a part of that group of kids standing over at the bar all evening?" Frank asked.

"Yes," Andrew said. "He was acting hostile, but I don't think he could have done this."

"Did any of you see him leave?" McGinty asked.

Everyone shook their heads no.

Frank looked thoughtful. "Do you think he might have done it for revenge?"

John caught the doubting tone in Frank's voice and defended his theory, "He was acting suspicious all day, like he knew something we didn't."

The detective said, "In high profile families such as yours, the motive for kidnapping is usually ransom."

"Remember, Andrew," John insisted, "how we were saying that he and his stealing friend felt entitled to help themselves to everything of yours?"

Judy came downstairs to tell them that Marie was finally asleep. She put her arms around her brother's shoulders in a silent embrace.

"John thinks one of our employees took Georgi for ransom money."

She sat down hard in the chair beside Andrew and stared at John incredulously. "You mean someone here, celebrating with us today did this and not some criminal off the street?"

"It's just a theory," Frank said.

"A theory that will be checked out," McGinty said. Motioning toward the two officers leaving the house, he said, "They're going to go find McPherson and question him."

The phone rang and they momentarily froze. All except for McGinty, that is, who calmly adjusted the dials on a device he had previously attached to the phone. Putting on a headset, he motioned for Andrew to pick up the receiver.

With shaking hands, Andrew picked it up, then slumped with relief when he heard Ted's familiar voice on the other end of the line, calling to give them an update on Denise and Mae's conditions. Turning to the table, he answered their questioning stares. "Ted said that they're releasing Denise but that she needs to stay calm, so they're going to a hotel rather than come back here tonight. Mae is still in a coma. Joe is staying there with her."

Judy got up and said, "It's going to be a long night.   I'll make some coffee."

PART TWO

Twenty-Three Years Later

Chapter Four

"Go wash your hands so you can help me shuck this corn for dinner," Mae said to Judy's two children, Henry (Hank), age twelve and Alice ("call me Ali, please"), age ten.

Ali, always exuberant to help her Gamma Mae, obeyed, while Hank remained on the veranda, absently kicking at a pebble that had strayed from one of the surrounding flowerbeds.

Mae was fairly tolerant of his moods. She knew the conflicts of a twelve-year old boy's hormones; wanting to remain a boy one minute, and yearning to be a man the next.

"What's the matter, Hank?" she asked him.

"Nothin'"

Ali ran back to join Mae, who was set up outside with the garbage can and bag of corn. "Can I cut out the worms, Gamma?" she asked.

"Well," Mae said, looking at Hank, "usually that's your brother's job, but if he doesn't want to do it…"

"I'll do it," Hank said, coming over to take a seat with them, secretly grateful for a reason to hang around, even though all Ali could talk about was her stupid birthday party tomorrow. The birthday party had been on his mind all day, and he couldn't hold his torment in any longer.

"Bobby's mom won't let him come to the party," he said angrily. Bobby was his new best friend at school. He had moved to town over the summer and since the first day of school, a mere month ago, they had been an inseparable team of two. "She says this house is cursed and she won't let him step foot in it."

"Fools like that make me want to do some cursing myself," Mae said under her breath. Out loud she asked, "You think our house is cursed, Hank?"

"No...but..."

"But it's all anyone ever talks about when they find out who we are or where we live," Ali said.

The Lexington Kidnapping. It was the town's most notorious legend.

"Yeah, smarty pants?" Hank asked. "Did anyone ever tell you they wouldn't come to your house for a stupid party because of it?" He got up so abruptly that his chair tipped backwards and he was running up the stairs before anyone could answer his rhetorical question.

He ran right past his mom, who was walking in the front door from work, and didn't even answer her greeting.

"What's the matter with Hank?" Judy asked when she came out onto the veranda.

"Hi Mom!" Ali said as Judy bent over to kiss her forehead. "Bobby's mom said our house is cursed and she won't let him come to my party."

Judy looked to Mae for confirmation and found her seething with anger. *What a stupid, idiotic thing to say to a little boy!* Judy thought.

Sighing, she picked up the toppled chair and sat down, absently playing with her car keys.

Judy had spent so much time at home in Pittsburg after the kidnapping, that she and her bosses decided she should open a sister clinic and move back permanently, which had pleased Mae no end.

Ali said, "Well you've said it yourself, Gamma, that those two old aunts put a curse on this family."

"That old curse ran itself out long ago," Mae said, not wanting to be reminded of the events of that fateful day. "A lot of good water's gone under the bridge since then."

"Like what?" Ali asked.

"For one thing, your mom and dad would have never gotten married if your mom hadn't moved back home," Mae said.

"Oh, I'm sure we would have worked out our difference in opinions eventually," John drawled, coming onto the veranda from the kitchen.

"Daddy!" Ali screamed, jumping up for her hug.

"And just what were our differences in opinions?" asked a grinning Judy, as John bent over to give her a kiss.

"More like what *didn't* you two squabble about," Mae harrumphed. "You two been fussin' since the day you laid eyes on each other. Took some real problems to pull out the love that was hiding in those spats."

Smiling sadly, Judy said, "Like you and Joe."

Gathering up the naked corn in her apron, Mae said, "That's how I knew. Come on, Ali, you can help me get supper ready while your mom and dad get out of their work clothes."

Judy asked John, "Would you talk to Hank? Bobby's mom said our house is cursed and she won't let him come to the party tomorrow. I'm too angry to be of much help to him right now."

"What kind of nonsense is that?" John asked, marching off to find his son.

Left alone on the veranda, Judy idly picked at gossamers of corn silk that had fled the garbage can, wondering again how the events of so long ago could haunt her children as they did. They hadn't even been conceived at the time! Hank and Ali had nothing to do with any of it, she thought angrily. Yet to this day, one of them would periodically come home from school upset about somebody's insensitive remarks.

The case file on the kidnapping had never been officially closed, and although most people still thought Seth McPherson was guilty, no definitive proof had been found. Theories and gossip and the events following that fateful night had fueled a legend that wasn't about to die.

Not like Joe, she thought. Or Marie, two more victims sacrificed on the altar of that legend.

That's what really made her angry; that they were all victims of one person's actions that had changed their lives forever. Every day she counseled women not to be a casualty of their circumstances, and yet felt helpless in her own family.

John came back outside and handed Judy a gin and tonic. Reading her thoughts, he said, "Don't be so hard on yourself," sitting down beside her and sipping his own drink. "You help me deal with it every day."

Looking gratefully at her husband, she said, "Dealing with what actually happened and the ghosts of it still haunting our children are two separate things."

John looked at her for a long moment before saying, "Someone very wise once told me ghosts only have the influence you give them."

She had to smile at that, for she had uttered those words. "You're my hero," she said fondly.

John had effectively knocked the self-pity out of her as she remembered the guilt he had to exorcise each time these memories surfaced.

She had first seen the depth of his loyalty to their family when a bitter and angry Seth McPherson showed up at their house several weeks after the kidnapping, yelling for Andrew to come outside. John told Andrew to stay put and went outside instead, trying to reason with Seth who was deranged with fury. The police had questioned him relentlessly, but they could find no evidence to arrest him. From the house, she heard Seth yell, "This whole town thinks I took her. You've ruined my life!" She and Mae warned Andrew not to go outside for the fight Seth so desperately wanted and were watching from the window as John tried to calm him down. They had called the police and Mae was begging God to make them hurry up and get there.

But Andrew couldn't be held back and tore out of the house to help John.

Setting his sights on Andrew, Seth pulled a knife from his jeans pocket and headed toward him, screaming at him to quit fucking with his life and threatening to tear him apart if the police questioned him one more time.

John never saw the knife. His attention had been diverted to Andrew when he burst out of the house.

But Joe had heard the commotion from the backyard and came around the house just in time to see Seth pull the jackknife out of his pocket and flick it open. Joe lunged at Seth while he was in mid-stride, consequently receiving the full wrath of Seth's frustration and rage. John and Andrew caught a few swipes of the blade as they fought to get Seth off of Joe, but by the time they were able to physically overpower Seth and restrain him, Joe was dead and Mae was on the ground wailing over him.

Andrew had been treated and released, but John was in the hospital with his wounds for almost a week. It was there, sitting by his bed while he convalesced, that Judy realized he wasn't the arrogant playboy she had believed him to be. In the weeks and months that followed, she allowed herself to fall in love with him.

Laughing, she said to him now, "Tell me again how you were more afraid of me than of Seth."

He embellished the story of the torch he had carried for her all those years he knew her as Andrew's little sister. How he had wanted, but had been too afraid, to approach her. "You had a fiery, sassy temper," he said. "Still do."

He saw the gleam in her eyes and asked, "Bet you want to show me right now just how sassy you are. Want to wrestle?"

"I have to go set the table for dinner or else I'd take you up on that offer," she winked. "I may be getting older, but I can still whoop you," she laughed at his mock disappointment and disappeared into the house.

That you can, John thought with a grin. She was a strong woman, but he wasn't thinking of her physical strength. 'Headstrong' is the way Mae so aptly described her. Judy had a way of tackling a problem and not letting go until it gave in to her. She had been his strength in those terrible months after the kidnapping and Joe's death. He still blamed himself, but as Judy kept telling him, that did neither him nor Joe any good.

He was the one who had insisted on Seth's guilt, and now, after all these years, he still didn't know if he had been right or wrong. Seth had been locked away for Joe's murder, but still adamant about his innocence in the kidnapping.

No evidence had been found; no legitimate ransom calls had been received. Seth would be a free man today if it hadn't been for Joe's death.

There had been several idle speculations about who else might have taken Georgi, a few leads, and even one confession from a deranged nut case, but all had turned into dead ends. The majority of the town still thought that Seth McPherson had taken Georgi for ransom, decided against it with the fever of publicity that ensued, and had dumped her body somewhere, never to be found.

Most everyone except Andrew, that is. John both respected and admired Andrew's faith that his daughter was still alive. He knew faith was what kept Andrew going and focused. He wished he had that faith.

He hated the questions and doubts that assailed him in those moments the picture of Seth attacking Joe replayed in his mind like a stuck tape. Those were the moments when he had to look to the example of his two best friends -- there was no room in Andrew or Judy's minds for guilt or blame. They shoved them aside and refused to drink that poison.

Poor Marie hadn't that constitution. She succumbed to grief and despair and had grown increasingly frail as the months stretched into years with no word about her daughter. There was hardly anything left of her at the end. Her body was ravaged by the sorrow that was eating away at her mind and heart.

Andrew was devastated, of course, but Marie's increasing frailness only strengthened his resolve to find Georgi. It gave him force and a purpose and John was hard put to keep up with him. There wasn't a day went by that Andrew wasn't taking out an ad in another newspaper or talking to someone on the phone about another plan to find her.

Between that and throwing himself into his work after Marie died, he was never home. So when John and Judy got married, Andrew surrendered the master suite in the house to them and took an apartment in town closer to work, against all of their protests.

TLC was doing better than ever and didn't require all those additional hours, but his work was his solace and he had built up an impressive empire, expanding its operations to plants and properties around the globe. Andrew had become a town hero since the kidnapping, an icon of fortitude and faith. Even after leads to finding Georgi had dried up and the police quit looking, Andrew pursued his own investigation by hiring private detectives and placing ads in papers all over the world with sketches of what Georgi might look like today.

As if his thoughts of Andrew had conjured him up, he heard Ali scream, "Uncle Drew!"

When John came into the kitchen to greet Andrew, he saw that Andrew's presence had brought Hank downstairs, all gloominess forgotten at the joy of seeing his favorite uncle.

"You're coming to my party tomorrow, aren't you Uncle Drew?" Ali asked.

"You bet I am," Andrew responded. "Being ten is a huge milestone! I wouldn't miss it for anything."

"Does that mean you're finally going to let me take a Saturday off?" John teased.

"Only because of the monumental importance of the occasion," Andrew teased back, giving John a good slug on the arm.

Noticing his overnight bag, Mae said, "You're staying, I hope. I've got your room all ready for you."

"You're the best," Andrew said, hugging her. "What's for dinner? I'm starving."

When they had finished eating and were sitting satiated around the table discussing last minute plans for the party, Mae got up and returned with an envelope.

"I hope this isn't another wild goose chase," she said, reluctantly handing the envelope to Andrew. "It came in the mail for you yesterday."

Everyone was silent as Andrew stared at it apprehensively. It was postmarked from California and had a return address from The Sisters of St. Mary Hospice.

"Open it!" Ali cried impatiently.

Carefully, so as not to tear into the postmark or insignia, he sliced the envelope with his butter knife, unfolded a single sheet of thin paper and read out loud:

Andrew:

I will get right to the point because I'm dying and I don't have much time left. If you want to hear what happened to your daughter, you better get here soon.

Mike Bigelow

Everyone was talking at once, but Andrew had tuned them out and was deep in thought about what he had just read. It had been several years since he had received an unsolicited letter or a call about his daughter. He had meticulously checked out each and every lead, even if he hadn't thought it legitimate, so there was no question about this one either. He knew that he would go talk to this man.

Just as everyone else around the table knew, and had suddenly grown quiet.

John bridged the silence by saying, "I'll go with you, Andrew."

Andrew looked around at his family. Mae had gotten up to make coffee, and he could only guess at the expression she was hiding. Judy was intensely interested in the food on her plate and was pushing it around with her fork. Ali was looking at him with disappointment written all over her little face. He didn't like doing this to them again, but he had no choice.

"Thanks, John. We'll go right after Ali's party tomorrow."

Watching the sunshine return to her eyes, he added, "I told you I wouldn't miss it for anything."

"I want to go with you," Hank announced.

Suddenly alert, Judy's look to John reflected the terror she felt. Andrew had come up against some crazy, desperate people in his search for Georgi. It was one thing to put himself in danger, but she didn't want her son exposed to those perils.

"I'm old enough!" he wailed, knowing what she was thinking.

"Your mother and I will discuss it later," John said to Hank. He wasn't sure what he thought about the idea, but he had other pressing matters on his mind at the moment. "In the meantime, I'm going to call Les McGinty and see if he has anything on this guy, Bigelow."

Chapter Five

Hank could hardly believe that his mom had relented! But here he was, on the plane that would take them to California. He felt so important at his sister's party, telling everyone that he was going in a plane all the way across the United States.

Surprisingly, Mae had been the one to tip the scales in his favor, saying if he was old enough to hear nonsense from his friends at school, then he was old enough to deal with real life.

His mom finally gave in when John and Andrew promised Hank would stay in the waiting room at the hospital.

The detective who had been in charge of the kidnapping case, Les McGinty, was now a captain on the force. He had refused to allow the department to close the case, and he helped Andrew with his search whenever he was able, ignoring his boss's protests. Over the years, he may have grown a small spare tire around his waist, but he still looked like he could take down several people at once, if only by intimidation. He met them at the airport and filled them in on what he had discovered about Mike Bigelow. He then surprised them with his decision to accompany them to California.

Reciting from his notes, he said, "Bigelow grew up in Pittsburgh, left home when he was seventeen, according to his mother. The last time she heard from him was when he told her he got married and moved to Ohio," Les said. "Our records show some petty stuff, typical small time hoodlum."

"So what about that is bringing you to California with us?" John asked.

Ignoring his question, Les continued, "I checked with Ohio records and they said his vehicle was registered in Port Clinton, Ohio, so I called the department there. They had several domestic violence calls from his wife, Patricia, but she never followed through with any of them and he dropped off the radar about 10 years ago."

"So…" started John again, but Les held up his hand to continue.

"Bieglow's mother-in-law told me Mike and Patricia had three daughters, the oldest one named Linda. She was born on September 10, 1961."

John gasped as Andrew's eyes bore into Les. "The day of the kidnapping," Andrew voiced what they all knew. "Does it say where she was born?"

"She said she was born in Pittsburgh," Les said, "but that's all the information we've got right now. My department is following up and I'll call them back later to see what they come up with."

"But get this, I checked Pittsburgh hospital records and couldn't find a recorded birth. However, I did find a death certificate for a baby girl named Linda Bigelow on the same day."

John let a whistle escape through his teeth.

In the stunned silence, Hank could no longer contain his questions, "What does that mean?" he asked.

Looking at the three of them, Les said, "This is all very preliminary and I don't know what it means yet, except that I want to talk to this guy. It could be just a coincidence, or it could be a typo for all I know."

Trying to make his mind focus on the facts, Andrew asked, "You didn't find a birth certificate for Linda Bigelow?"

"Not yet," Les said.

"But you do have record of a very much alive Linda Bigelow?" John said, stunned at the implications.

~ ~ ~ ~

Andrew was staring out of the plane window into the black night sky, trying to untangle his conflicting emotions. Relief and hope and dread were knotted together in the place where his heart should have been. He was trying very hard not to imagine what his little girl's life would have been like, raised by a thieving, lying, wife-beating, criminal, and willing his mind to focus on his questions for Bigelow instead. He had to find her and he couldn't let himself cave into these kinds of thoughts. *Focus*, he demanded his charged nerves and brain.

"We'll go talk to this guy first thing in the morning," he said to the excited and fidgety Hank, hoping that Bigelow hadn't died since he had penned the letter and that they weren't too late.

~ ~ ~ ~

The hospice looked more like a nursing home than a hospital, Andrew thought when they arrived. Except that there were young people, as well as old, sitting around the main "living" area, watching TV or playing cards, waiting out their end of days. Bright suns were drawn on the walls, trying desperately to dispel the gloom, but came up sorely lacking.

"Oh yes, I do believe Mr. Bigelow has been expecting you," the nurse who was on duty at the front desk said. "I'll bring his roommate out here to play checkers with this young man," she winked at Hank. Judy had called ahead to make arrangements for someone to watch Hank while John and Andrew talked to Bigelow. "Mr. Will just loves playing that game."

Once they got Hank set up and were assured that the nurse would keep an eye on him from the desk, they walked to Room 35, as instructed, and found a man who looked like he was 90 years old, shriveled up and wasted. Did they have the wrong room? They were expecting someone approximately 55 years old. They were preparing to leave when the corpse opened his eyes and assessed his guests. Those eyes were the only part of his anatomy clinging to life, glinting with painful determination.

"No need for your bodyguards, Lexington," he said, dispelling their doubts of viability. "I'm afraid I'm not much of a threat to you anymore."

Les introduced himself and said, "I'd like to ask you some questions, Mr. Bigelow."

Mike received this announcement with a frown and said, "I don't have much time, Captain. After I tell Andrew here what I want to tell him, I'll answer your questions. I will tell you, though, that you guys had it all wrong about Seth."

"Did you know Seth McPherson?" Les persisted in his inquiry.

"I knew him in high school," Mike said, "but he didn't take your daughter, Andrew. I let him take the rap for it, but he had nothing to do with it – except to tell me about your party."

Andrew stopped him, wanting to assure himself of the validity of his story. "Just so we know if you're telling the truth, does my daughter have any distinguishing marks on her, Bigelow?"

"I never put any marks on her, if that's what you're insinuating," Mike bristled.

"He doesn't mean man-made marks, you idiot," John seethed.

After some thought, which seemed to take months, rather than moments to endure, Mike said, "Oh yeah, she had a birthmark – on her butt."

The three men were still standing by the door, but when Andrew heard this, he made a lunge for the bed. Les and John restrained him, and John said, "Let's hear him out, Drew. We have to find out where she is."

"What do you mean 'had'? What did you do with my daughter?" Andrew was forcing himself to calm down.

"She's still alive, if that's what you mean," Mike said.

Twenty-three years of dread and pent-up fear abruptly drained from Andrew's body with the news that his daughter was alive, and he probably would have slumped to the floor had John not still been holding onto him.

Les said, "Okay Bigelow, it's your time to shine. Tell us what we came to hear."

Taking his good old time and wrenching Andrew's patience, he began, "I saw Seth that day. I was in a bar after my wife had a dead baby, trying to figure out how I was going to tell her."

"Your wife, Patricia?" Les asked.

"Yes," Mike said. "Only she doesn't know anything about this, I never told her. Never told anyone."

"That's a little far-fetched, Bigelow," Les said. "You mean to say she just took this baby believing it was hers?"

"Do you want to hear the story or not?" Mike asked.

The three of them nodded for him to continue.

"I knew it was a mistake from the moment Pat told me she just had to go home for her old man's funeral. But she wouldn't listen to me when I told her that the trip would be a disaster, and that she shouldn't travel in her condition. Her doctor even told her she shouldn't go, but she wasn't listening to anyone.

Mike was caught up in his memories. "That family is nuts. All of them. No sooner did we get there, then they start interfering and upsetting Patty so much that her brother ends up taking her to the hospital in the middle of the night – all behind my back. They never did have no respect for me as her husband. They just take over her life like I don't even exist."

He stalled to ruminate on past injustices and Les asked, "What is your wife's maiden name?"

The question seemed to nudge the sick man out of his daydream and he continued with his story.

"Anyways, I come downstairs the next morning and no one would even acknowledge I was standing there. I ask 'where is Patty,' and they all clam up tight and scurry about pretending they're busy, not even looking at me. So I start looking around for Patty myself, to tell her that we're packing up our shit and getting the hell out of there, when I run into her brother coming out of the bathroom. The meddling SOB tells me that he took Patty to the hospital in the middle of the night, just like that. Hadn't asked for my permission or even told me about it. He's going on about how it was an emergency and all, but all I could think was how they always looked down their noses at me, like I wasn't good enough for their Patty. Like I was pond scum and they were the fucking water lilies or something. So I told him they could all go fuck themselves and I put our suitcases in the car and got the hell out of there.

I was thinking her family was damn well going to pay for this little hospital visit when I got to her room and saw her sitting there, all by herself, crying. Patty never cried. Well, not since she found out how pissed off it makes me. But coming up on her and surprising her like that, I couldn't believe how sad she looked. When she saw me, she acted like she was scared of me! That's the kind of ideas those people put in her head and it made me mad all over again.

She asks me 'What's wrong?' like she don't know and then starts crying again when I tell her she's the one who has some explaining to do. She says that the doctor thinks she could lose the baby and she's crying to beat the band.

I tell her to quit it, everything's going to be all right, when all of a sudden she grabs at her stomach and screams. I could tell she wasn't faking it, and I got scared too. I rang the call bell for the nurse and the old battleax comes in and glares at me, like it was all my fault or something. She checks Patty's pulse and then makes me leave the room! Said they were taking Patty to surgery. All I could do was to call to Patty as they were wheeling her away and tell her that everything was going to be all right. Man, that look she gave me then. The look she used to give me back when we were dating, like I was her hero. Like she trusted me."

His voice trailed off again and Andrew impatiently brought him back to his story, not wanting to risk his dying before he could get the whole story out of him. "So your baby dies and you take mine," Andrew said bitterly.

"How did your wife not know?" John was incredulous.

But now that his time of reckoning had come, Mike wasn't about to be shortchanged in his attempt at absolution.

"So I paced for hours in the waiting room," he continued. "I couldn't believe that I was so upset about the chance of losing that baby. I didn't want a baby, didn't even want Patty to keep it when she told me she was pregnant. But she was so happy and excited that I kind of got caught up with it too, I guess. I never had no family to speak of. My old man took off when I was eight and my mom was too busy taking care of herself to pay me or my sister any mind. I was always babysitting my little sister while our mother was out 'trying to find us a new father,' as she put it."

"If Patty lost this baby, she was going to be miserable to live with for God knew how long. The one thing I can't stand is to listen to her crying day after day. It reminds me too much of my little sister crying for our mother night after night and me not being able to do a damn thing about it."

"Then the doctor came out and said that Patty was in recovery, that she was fine but he couldn't save the baby, a little girl. He said that the placenta broke away from the uterus and the baby had died before she had a chance to be born. Then he asked me the baby's name and I tried to remember what girl names Patty had tossed out and said the first one that came to my mind. I told him Linda."

"I wanted to see Patty, but the doctor said she'd been heavily sedated and that she would sleep until morning. I asked him if she knew about the baby dying and he said no, we would tell her together in the morning. So I went in to check on her before I left and she was sleeping so peaceful. I had promised her that everything would be all right and she had trusted me. That news was going to destroy her and the last shred of trust she had in me. She would never again give me that look."

Ignoring the incredulous stares on their faces, he continued. "So I left the hospital and went to the bar around the corner to sort out my thoughts. I was sitting there drinking a beer when Seth comes in. I hadn't seen him since high school. We talked about old times for a while and he told me that he just came from your house for your daughter's party.

He was telling me all about your palace and how much money you had and how arrogant you were. He told me you just put his buddy in jail for some hopped up charge of embezzlement. He was pretty bitter and I guess he got me worked up to thinking about how much you had and how little I had. How you've been handed everything on a silver platter and how hard I worked .... It just wasn't fair."

Andrew had heard enough. "You son of a bitch," he started toward the bed again, but Les put out a restraining arm. "Let's get his full confession," Les said, "and then I will conveniently look the other way."

"I just got to thinking how easy it would be to show up at your party and act like a guest and check things out. That's all I was going to do, but when I walked in the front door, no one was in the house. I was about to go out the back door and maybe grab something to eat, when your maid started up the steps with the baby. She was a little thing – sure looked like a newborn to me – and then something just took over, like instinct. I ran upstairs and hid behind the nursery door."

"I just don't get how you made the switch for a dead baby and your wife never knew," John said again, fixated on that point.

"She was all drugged up when I got to the hospital," Mike said. "She didn't know nothing. I put her in a wheelchair and put a pillow in her arms, told her it was her baby, and she never knew the difference. The ambulance with your maid was just getting there then and everyone was busy talking about what had happened. No one paid any attention to us."

Andrew shuddered at the thought that he had almost killed Mae, had fractured her skull.

"Where was Georgi during all this?" Les asked.

"In the car sleeping. She and Patty slept most of the way back home to Ohio."

"Where is she now?" Andrew asked.

"I don't know where she is," Mike said. I haven't seen or talked to her in over ten years."

Mike gazed out of the window and continued on slowly, remembering. "She was a sweet little girl. She just adored me and followed me around everywhere I went. Patty had grown cold and hard over the years. Could have been partly my fault, I guess. I had this secret about what I done."

Turning his head back to face them, he said, "Anyway, she kicked me out and I haven't seen any of them since. After all I did for that woman, she still blames me for her messed up life. I risked everything for her. I risked going to jail just to shut her up and make her happy."

Andrew was spent. His anger had dissipated into a pool of regret that his daughter's life had been ambushed for such pitiful reasons. This man, even on his deathbed confession, was blaming others for his actions.

"You're an animal," he growled as he walked towards the bed. He was staring into the darkest eyes he had ever seen, the depth of which descended to hell itself. "Have you no conception of how many lives you've stolen?"

Bigelow pulled a small pistol out from under the bedcovers and aimed it at Andrew, pausing his stride. The split-second lapse was just long enough for Mike to say, "I ain't proud of what I did. Tell Linda I'm sorry."

He turned the gun to his own head and fired before anyone had a chance to move.

~ ~ ~ ~

As soon as John snapped out of his shock and realized Andrew wasn't hit, he ran to the waiting room, lamenting that Judy had been right – oh, how he regretted bringing Hank with them.

Hank was frozen to the spot where John had left him, eyes wide with terror from the sound of gunshot and people all around him screaming and running in different directions. When he saw his dad coming towards him, he began to shake and cry with relief. "Is Uncle Drew dead?" he asked while clinging to his dad for dear life.

"No, honey, he's fine." John said. "Bigelow shot himself. Uncle Drew wasn't hurt."

"Bigelow shot himself?" Mike's roommate, who had also been frozen to his spot at the game table, asked. Then anxious to repeat what he had heard from John, he quickly wheeled himself over to join the growing crowd of people at the door to his room who were trying to get a glimpse of Bigelow.

Hank was gaining control of himself and would certainly never tell anyone that he had cried like a baby. "Is he the guy who took Georgi?" he asked, wiping his nose on his sleeve.

"We still don't have any real proof, but it kind of looks that way. If he was telling the truth, Georgi may still be alive," John said.

"Uncle Drew was right!" Hank exclaimed.

"I certainly hope so, Hank," John said.

The police were arriving and moving everyone away from the bedroom door. John was extremely grateful that Les had insisted on coming with them and had witnessed that scene. Who knows what they would have been accused of if he and Andrew had been the only ones in that room. Let alone the fact that he would not have been able to hold Andrew off Bigelow alone. Not that he didn't want to kill the bastard himself, but it could have turned out a whole lot differently if Andrew had gotten to him a split second sooner.

"Hank," he said, "they're going to want to take my statement. Are you going to be all right here?"

"Of course, Dad," Hank said, like the grown-up he was becoming.

"Then stay right here, I'll be back as soon as I can," John said, giving him a hug.

John was more concerned about making sure Andrew cleaned himself up before Hank saw him than he was about a statement. *Judy is going to kill me*, he thought morosely.

Hank sat back down at the table and watched all the activity going on. He couldn't believe that he was seeing things he watched on TV happening in real life. The police were moving people away from the scene of the crime where his dad and uncle had seen a man shoot himself!

He must have taken Georgi, Hank thought. *Why else would you feel so bad that you would have to shoot yourself?* Something else was tickling his mind and he tried to think what it was. . . blood, that man's blood.

"Dad!" Hank called out. He had to get through the circle of people still milling around the bedroom door. He could see his dad right inside the door talking to a policeman and he called again, "Dad!"

John broke away, asking, "What's the matter, Hank?"

Hank was excited now and stammered, "Dad, remember the other night when you were telling us about that new invention you're testing at your work? The one that uses blood to tell if people are related?"

"Yes," John said slowly, trying to make his mind go back to their real, everyday lives when he would go to work and then come home and eat dinner. "That was a prototype of a DNA test that Robert is working on."

"Don't you see, Dad?" Hank said, "You could get some of that guy's blood and test it!"

"Hank, you're a genius!" John exclaimed. "Thanks for reminding me." He wasn't yet convinced of the accuracy of this new machine, but it was worth a try. "My boy," he said to a proud Hank, ruffling his hair.

~ ~ ~ ~

With all the commotion and delays at the hospital, they had missed their flight back to Pittsburgh and were waiting in the airport restaurant for the next flight out. Hank and Les were the only ones with appetites and were eating with gusto.

"Here, Hank, eat mine too," Andrew said. "We can't let you go back hungry. Your mom's going to have our hides as it is."

"Why aren't you coming back with us Uncle Drew?" Hank asked between bites.

"I've got some loose ends to tie up here," Andrew explained. He had decided to stay and find out what they were going to do with the body; whether they would ship Bigelow back to his wife for burial or bury him in California. Andrew wanted to be here on the off chance there was a funeral and that Georgi might attend.

"You tell your mom I'm very glad you were here," Andrew said. "If it weren't for you, we wouldn't have thought to get blood samples."

"Not to mention your detective work with Bigelow's roommate," Les winked. "We could use you on the force."

When they had been ruminating on where Bigelow could have gotten a gun, Hank remembered that Mr. Will had told him that Bigelow's wife had been in to visit just the week before but that Bigelow hadn't had any visitors before that or since.

"We're a team," Hank said importantly. "That's why you should come back with us, Uncle Drew."

"This team has to split up now to follow the leads," Les said. "I'll find out everything I can on Pat and Linda Bigelow, Andrew. Then as soon as you get back, assuming you don't meet up with them here, we'll go pay them a visit."

Chapter Six

Linda Bigelow woke up with a killer hangover. She knew she had to get herself together and go to work. Her boss was getting pretty tired of her calling in sick. *He's not the only one who's tired*, she thought plaintively. *Twenty-three years old and I'm just plain old tired.*

She was a secretary in a bank and when she called in sick, the other secretaries had to fill in for her. They were all friends, but she could tell they were getting annoyed with her absences.

I'm just getting too old to go out partying on a work night, she admonished herself, downing several aspirin with her coffee. Lowering herself gingerly onto a chair at her kitchen table, she lit a cigarette and stared out of the window at the car dealership parking lot beside her apartment building.

She needed her job. This was her first apartment all to herself and she loved her independence. She had gotten married when she was eighteen, more to get out of her mother's house than for any other reason. But that had only lasted a few years before her then-husband decided he would rather be with his former girlfriend from high school than with her.

It hadn't broken her heart, and that realization showed her she hadn't loved him like she had thought. Her ex-husband's apathy toward her bothered her less than her mother's "*I told you so.*"

No way was she going to move back home, even if she lost her job. She and her mother were like two wrong ends of a magnet, always pushing each other away, even though "family obligation" kept them both trying. *Pretending*, was more like it, she thought.

Her two younger sisters weren't all that close to her mom either; her mom didn't let anyone get very close. But her sisters didn't butt heads with her the way Linda always seemed to - without even trying. Their mother wasn't cruel to them either, like she could be to Linda. She had no idea why her mother was so angry with her all the time. But then, her mother was an angry person.

Why the heck am I thinking about my mother this morning, anyway? she wondered.

It was probably because of the guy she had brought home from the bar last night, she reasoned, knowing what her mother would have to say if she knew. He had left sometime in the night, thank God. Probably married. The ones who stick around until morning are usually single but then she had the additional penance of kicking them out.

She knew it was stupid, even dangerous, to bring guys home like that, but she never thought about that until the next morning when nursing a hangover. Then the self-reproach would pound in her head, along with the words of her mother: *you're a whore, a slut, a tramp.*

It wasn't sex she was looking for; but sex was the price paid for her to feel wanted and loved. Like an addiction, she craved the look in a man's eyes that told her she was pretty, sexy . . . wanted.

Abstractly, she knew she was pretty. It was her long, curly, sandy-colored hair that turned guys on, as well as her pretty face and small-boned, trim body. But she didn't feel attractive until she saw the look of desire in a man's eyes.

She yearned to find a man who would love her and look at her in the morning the way he had looked at her the night before.

No sense in crying over spilled milk, as her grandmother would say. She got up to take a shower and get ready for work.

She heard the phone ringing as she toweled herself off and ran to get it. Trying unsuccessfully to disguise the disappointment in her voice, she answered her mother's "good morning." *She probably knows about that guy that was here*, she thought, not putting it past her mother to have x-ray eyes into her apartment.

Her mother got right to the point, as usual, and said succinctly. "Your father died yesterday."

"What?"

"There's not going to be a funeral. I can't afford to have him shipped back here from California, so they're going to cremate him there."

Linda was at a loss as to what to say and her head was pounding with a vengeance now. Her mother hadn't mentioned her father in over ten years, not since the day he had left them. She could remember that day like it was yesterday. It had grooved a rut in the grey matter of her brain, and a record needle of her mother's words kept getting stuck in that groove, playing them over and over again.

Her dad had set her and her sisters down on the front porch to tell them he was going away. Linda had become hysterical, grabbing his legs as he tried to walk down the stairs and out of their lives. He told her he was moving to California and promised that he would be back to get her once he got settled. But he had never come back and she hadn't heard from him since. For all appearances, her mother had been right when she had viciously spat, "He didn't love you, you know," when Linda came into the house, sobbing, after he drove away.

Linda sat back down at the kitchen table and lit a cigarette with shaking hands. She still felt like a shell-shocked little girl when she thought about him. She had virtually no memory of her life before that day when he left them, just wisps of dream-like images. But her collective feeling from that time was that he was the only one in the family who paid her any attention at all. She felt like she was always defending him to her mother when he and her mother got into their fights and also defending herself for loving him.

"How did he die?" her voice cracked.

"He's had stomach cancer for years, no one expected him to last this long," her mother said dismissively.

"You knew he was sick?" Linda asked, sick to her stomach now, too.

"Of course I didn't," her mother said impatiently. "That's what they told me when they called this morning."

"Where is he, I want to go see him," Linda said.

"I told you," her mother said as if she were an obstinate child, "there will be no funeral."

"Still . . ." Linda said, "I'd like to see him."

"I don't know where he is," her mother said. "I told them to cremate him, and for all I know, that's already been done."

"But". . . Linda started again.

"Listen," her mother said. "I just thought that you'd want to know. I've got to go to work and so do you. Goodbye, Linda."

Chapter Seven

Andrew arrived at the airport an hour before his flight to Pittsburgh boarded and was trying to call Les to ask about the investigation. It had been a dead end in California and he was really hoping that Les had more information than he himself had been able to obtain. No answer.

Fortunately, though, he caught John at the office and vented his frustration at having wasted two days in California. "The guy had no friends and no visitors, other than his wife the week before," he told John. "If I didn't hate him so much, I'd almost pity him. The only information I was able to get is his wife's address."

"We got that too," John said. "But get this...her brother works for us."

"What? Who?" Andrew's mind was racing.

John knew there was no way of softening the blow, so he just came out with it. "Robert," he said to total silence on the other end of the line.

John still couldn't believe that "their" loyal and trustworthy Robert was in any way connected with Georgi's kidnapping. The guy John had trusted and mentored to help him with the day-to-day operations of TLC, as Andrew continued to expand the business and give John more of the operational responsibility. But facts were facts. He felt oddly responsible.

"Do you think we were set up?" Andrew asked eventually, not knowing what to make of this news. To think that someone right under their noses had been hiding this secret from them was making him shake with rage. "Robert knows as well as you do what I've gone through to find her!" Andrew exploded. "How could he possibly stand by and keep his mouth shut?"

"I could be wrong," John said, "but I don't think he knew. When I talked to him, he was as shocked as we are."

"How could he not know?"

"He confirmed a lot of the things we already knew, as well as the story Bigelow told us. He said that his father's funeral was the same day as Georgi's christening, which we knew. His sister and Bigelow had driven in from Ohio the day before, which is what Bigelow said. We just didn't realize the funeral Bigelow was talking about was Robert's father! Robert confirmed that his sister was pregnant and having some problems and that Bigelow refused to take her to the hospital. Robert ended up taking her to the emergency room in the middle of the night because she was bleeding and in a lot of pain. Bigelow went ballistic when he found out and told them all where to go and left the house. Robert and the rest of his family were busy with the funeral that day and no one went to the hospital, thinking they would go the next day. But that evening, Pat called from a rest stop on the turnpike to say that she had a baby girl and they were driving back to Ohio. She sounded groggy but happy. He said there was no reason to suspect anything except that Mike's bull-head was going to make it difficult to see his new niece because he refused to bring her to the house.

"That corroborates what that bastard told us," Andrew admitted. "But when he heard about the kidnapping, didn't he put two and two together?"

"Robert said they didn't turn on the TV the day of the funeral. He saw the news in the paper the next day, and that's when he came over to the house to see if there was anything he could do to help, remember? But none of them ever speculated that it might have anything to do with his brother-in-law. He said Mike was rough around the edges and that they all thought Pat had made a big mistake in marrying him, but Robert said he never would have dreamed he was capable of kidnapping. And even if he were, he said that Patty would never in a million years have gone along with it."

"He's insisting it's a huge mistake," John continued, "That maybe the drugs or the cancer got to Bigelow's brain and he made up the whole story. I'm sure he's worried about his job too, but Bigelow's story fits together too well to be a mistake, in my opinion. Robert is clutching at denial."

"Did you ask him about Linda?" Andrew asked.

"I did," John said. "He said that his sister has not kept close ties with the family and he didn't know where Linda was living now. But he gave me his sister's address. He didn't know anything about her birthmark."

Andrew thought about this a minute. Out loud he said, "But Bigelow did and I don't see how he could have made that up."

"Robert's theory is that Bigelow was closer to Seth McPherson than he let on and that he heard about the details of the kidnapping from Seth," John said. "Robert thinks that in Bigelow's drug-induced delirium, he might be rewriting history."

"Those are some powerful drugs if that was what he was doing," Andrew said. "Even if Bigelow were trying to clear Seth's name and take the rap for him, why do that now, when Seth is in jail for murdering Joe?"

"Robert is adamant that the DNA test will prove that Bigelow is Linda's biological father," John said. Les talked to him too, and his story was consistent with what he told me. He's beside himself. Not just about losing his job, but that his family would be implicated in this and that you would think he deceived you. He's agreed that he won't talk to his sister or anyone else in his family until after we've had a chance to talk to them – and he asked in turn that we not tell anyone about our suspicions until we find the truth."

"His ignorance of the whole thing seems pretty legit to me," John said, "but you can talk to him tomorrow and see what you think."

"I haven't been able to get a hold of Les," Andrew said. "Has he found Linda's address?

"Last I heard, he hadn't," John said.

"Do you know when we can go talk to Bigelow's wife? Andrew persevered. "She might refuse to talk to me alone, but she can't refuse an official investigation."

"Les is really kicking himself over this," John said, "thinking he slipped up somewhere and missed this angle. He wants to go as soon as you get back. Why don't you come over for dinner when you get off the plane? Judy is dying to talk to you."

"That sounds good," Andrew said. "I've been going crazy these last few days thinking about what my little girl might have gone through."

"I know." John said. "Thinking about it in the abstract is bad enough, but talking to Bigelow gave me the creeps."

"I'm wondering about Patricia, too." Andrew said. "Even if Bigelow pulled off the switch in the beginning, wouldn't a mother just know somehow that it wasn't her own child?"

"That's what Judy thinks," John said, "that she had to realize somewhere along the line that things weren't as they seemed. She wants to go with you when you talk to Pat."

~ ~ ~ ~

After talking to Robert in his office the next day, Andrew was coming to the same conclusion as John. The guy seemed sincere and told him what he had told John and Les, although Robert was convinced more than ever that the kidnapper was actually Seth, the connection between Seth and Mike being too coincidental.

"I'm not defending Mike," Robert emphasized. "I never trusted the guy and hated the way he treated my sister. But she loved him, still does. It makes me crazy the way she's pined over him all these years. If the DNA test comes back showing Mike wasn't Linda's biological father, then I will do everything in my power to get to the bottom of this and find out the truth," he promised.

"Bigelow said that Pat kicked him out," Andrew said. "Do you know why?"

Robert gave a snort. "If she kicked him out, I'd have a whole lot more respect for her. But she told me that he left her. I've believed that because that's how she's acted all these years, like she was the one left behind. The guy separated her from her family, drank, beat her up, ran around, couldn't keep a job, leaves her, and she still loves and defends him. I've never understood it."

"They never got divorced?" Andrew asked. "Even though they were separated for over ten years?"

"Not that I ever heard," Robert said. "Patty would get enraged if we even brought up the "D" word. Said we were trying to split up her family. So we quit."

"What about Linda?" Andrew asked. "If your sister found out, or guessed, that Linda wasn't her daughter, would she have said anything to you or your mother?"

"No, and I'm positive of that. Mike succeeded in putting a wedge between us all," Robert said. "Besides, Patty is proud and stubborn and if she found out something that horrible, I know she would never tell anyone. But I've never seen any indication she thought that." He thought a few minutes and added, "Patty has always been a little harder on Linda than the other two girls I guess, but Linda was her firstborn and you're always hardest on them."

"What do you mean?" Andrew asked.

"Well, Linda's always been such a sweet, quiet little girl, introverted to the point you'd have to pry the words out of her. She's always been my favorite niece," Robert smiled shyly. "But Patty was always harping on her about one thing or another, as if Linda was this troublesome kid or something and I never got that."

"How was your brother-in-law's relationship with Linda?" Andrew asked.

"I never saw Mike again after the day he stormed out of our house," Robert said. "When Patty visited, it was just her and the kids, and when we went there, Mike made himself scarce. So I never saw him with the kids, but I get the impression that Linda was Mike's favorite too, and it used to really piss Patty off. Although I've never been able to picture Mike being kind to anyone."

"So what's your theory on why Mike would call me out there for this deathbed confession if it wasn't true?" Andrew asked.

Robert was silent a moment, then said, "You know, at first I was shocked . . . and scared that it might be true. But the more I think about it, the more it doesn't surprise me at all. Mike was always stirring up trouble, just for the hell of it, it seemed. I guess I don't see him as being so noble as to clear Seth's name. Maybe this was his way of slamming Patty one last time. Along with her family. And maybe I'm telling myself this because I can't bear to think that it may be true."

"I have a daughter, Andrew," he said, getting choked up and having to pause a minute before continuing. "If I thought for one second that he had done this, I would have gone to Cleveland and killed the bastard myself."

John was in Andrew's office the second Robert vacated it, wanting to know Andrew's impression.

"I tend to agree with you, John. He seems sincere. Even so, I don't want him involved in the DNA testing. He's got too much at stake."

"We'll send Scott to the Michigan plant to do the tests," John said. "That way we'll know for sure that Robert hasn't been anywhere near the test or the results. Speaking of which, stop by the lab and let Scott draw some blood before you leave for Ohio."

"Now we just have to find Georgi," Andrew said, picking up his briefcase.

Chapter Eight

Pat Bigelow woke up determined she wasn't going to spend another day wrapped up in thoughts of the past. Thinking was the root of all her problems, she decided, as she stabbed bobby pins into her dark brown hair, securing it into a tight French twist. She avoided looking in the mirror in front of her; hated that haggard stranger's face that looked back at her with accusing eyes and a perpetual scowl. When she happened to catch a glimpse of herself, it reminded her of how pretty she used to be; how those eyes used to sparkle with so much life and hope. Now all that sparked was anger and resentment.

It was Saturday morning and the weekend stretched out before her like a chasm she had to breach. She dreaded the days when her work as a secretary didn't fill the hours and her mind with her responsibility and duties. Her tears had dried up and left her long ago, and took with them any hope that her life would ever change. She was left with a fierce determination that she would hold her head up high and make the best of the cards she had been dealt.

She had a decent house, though a rental, it was still the nicest house she had lived in since moving out of her parents' home. She had a decent job that paid the bills, and she had raised three daughters on her own. She had reason to be proud.

Today she was going to paint her living room. She attacked it as on a mission to cover over the dirt and grime of the past with a fresh coat of summer yellow. She was only fifty-two years old. Too young to feel like her life was over. Everyone had regrets, and the trick was not to let them overtake you; to keep walking forward and not look back.

Mike was dead. Gone forever, and gone with him was any thread of hope for a miracle. It was a relief, really. That hope had grown heavier and harder to carry as the years went by and now she was free of it. Free of any thoughts that he might come to his senses and realize how much he loved and needed her.

She had tried to tell him, had written him so many letters saying that he could so easily wipe out the past and undo all the hurt. She had forgiven him and loved him. But in the end, she had granted him his last wish and had given up her own.

She hadn't been sure she was going to give him the handgun until she got there and saw how pathetic he was and that he hadn't been lying about death being imminent. He told her he loved her but some things couldn't be undone; it was their same old argument. Sitting there holding his hand and looking at his wasted body, the fight left her. It was too late.

Now who could be knocking on her door this early in the morning? she thought, climbing down from the ladder and balancing her paintbrush on the edge of the paint can.

"Patricia Bigelow?" Les asked, showing his badge.

"What is it?" Pat looked in alarm at the three people standing on her porch.

Les introduced Andrew and Judy and asked if they could ask her a few questions.

She was trying to remember where she had heard the name, Lexington, before, but she couldn't place it.

"What is it?" she asked again.

"It's about Linda. May we come in?" the policeman asked.

Standing aside so they could enter, Pat asked, "Oh my God, what has she done now?" inwardly breathing a sigh of relief this wasn't about Mike shooting himself with the gun she had given him.

"Done?" Les asked. "No, it's nothing like that, Mrs. Bigelow."

"We'll have to go into the dining room," Pat said. "As you can see, I've got the living room torn up. I haven't got much time, the paint is drying as we speak."

"Then we'll come right to the point," Les said, easing himself carefully into one of the fragile looking dining room chairs. Judy and Andrew did the same.

"My daughter was kidnapped," Andrew explained, "the same day your daughter was born."

Of course, thought Pat, *that's where she had heard the name.* "Yes, I remember now. I was very sorry to hear that, especially having a brand new baby myself. I was terrified that someone would try to take her. But. . .what does this have to do with Linda?"

"Can you tell us about Linda's birth?" Les asked.

"Her birth?" Pat asked incredulously. "Why?"

"In what hospital was she born?" Les ignored her question.

"Marymount Medical Center, why?" she asked again.

"Did you know there was no birth certificate for a Bigelow baby that day?"

"Why of course there was," Pat said in a huff. "I've got a copy of it. Linda has the original."

"May we see it?" Andrew asked.

None of them spoke as Pat went upstairs to retrieve the certificate, coming back and setting it firmly on the table in front of Andrew with an air of finality. "I'm sorry for your loss, Mr. Lexington, but Linda is not your daughter, if that's what you're implying."

Les was examining the certificate, writing some notes in his book. Taking another piece of paper out of his briefcase, he said, "Then how would you explain this death certificate we found for Linda Bigelow filed by Marymount Medical Center on September 10, 1961?"

Stunned, Pat stared at the paper as if it were a snapping turtle waiting for her to extend her finger.

"It has to be a mistake," she said at last.

Les put the two papers side by side and pointed to the death certificate. "This one has the hospital insignia on it," he said. "It's missing from the birth certificate. Plus, the state seal is all wrong."

"Well, like I said, mistakes do happen," she trailed off. She was remembering when she had asked Mike for Linda's birth certificate. He was vague, saying he would get it for her. But months went by before he finally produced it to stop her nagging. "Things were so rushed that night," she said.

"Can you tell us about Linda's birth?" Les asked.

"Let's see," she said, thinking back. "I went into the hospital early in the morning on the tenth. My brother took me in because I was having contractions. We were visiting my family. My father's funeral was that day but I missed it," she said wistfully. "Instead, I got my Linda," she looked pointedly at Andrew.

"What happened when you got to the hospital?" Les asked.

"Nothing unusual," she said. "They were monitoring my contractions and gave me something to ease the pain. I don't remember much after that."

"Do you remember the delivery at all?" Judy asked.

"I remember the pain, until the drugs kicked in. I remember the doctor and nurses standing around me, but I couldn't make out anything they were saying. Their mouths were moving but nothing was coming out. Then I went to sleep."

"What about when you woke up?" Judy asked.

"My husband was taking us home," Pat said. "I was very drowsy, but I remember getting into the car and someone putting Linda into my lap. She was asleep and so beautiful," she smiled. "I fell asleep again, and when I woke up we were almost home."

"Did you think your baby was extremely well developed for a preemie?" Les asked.

She was getting irritated with this line of questioning. "No, I did not," she said. "My doctor had misjudged my due date." That's what Mike had told her.

"Why would your husband take you out of the hospital without a release from your doctor?" Les asked.

"He had a fight with my family," she said dismissively. "He wanted to get home. He was mad we went to Pittsburgh in the first place." She stood up and said, "I'm sorry I can't help you, but I must get back to my painting."

Andrew stood up as well and faced her, "Does Linda have a birthmark on her bottom left cheek?"

Pat looked at the three sets of eyes trained on her. She felt as if the floor were dropping away underneath her. She put her hand on the back of the chair to steady herself.

"Linda is not your daughter, Andrew," she said slowly, enunciating each word.

"I'd like to talk to her."

"That would do no good," Pat said. "She obviously does not remember anything about her birth."

"Do I need to remind you that we're investigating a kidnapping," Les said, interrupting the tense exchange.

"You can call it 'investigating' if you like, but I won't subject Linda to this harassment," Pat said. "It's time for you to leave."

"Your husband confessed to kidnapping Andrew's daughter," Les said, stopping Pat in mid-turn to where she was headed to show them out the door.

"That's a lie," she hissed, turning back angrily to look Les in the eye. "He did no such thing."

"He did," Les said. "Right before he killed himself with the gun you gave him."

Pat allowed herself to sit down before her legs gave out, but kept her spine rigid and her chin up. She would not lose her self-control in front of these people. She had spent a lifetime keeping the door to the past barred from her conscious thinking, knowing that if she opened it a crack, the demons would overtake her. How dare they come here, barging down that door and exposing her pain and suspicions.

"That's where you're wrong," she said to them. "I haven't seen my husband in ten years."

"We found the letters you sent him," Andrew said, "and we know you were there to visit him a week before he killed himself."

Pat had grown still and pale, but now she stood up again and said crisply, "Mike was obviously quite mad at the end. And for whatever reason he felt a need to 'confess' all those lies, we'll just never know. But unless you're going to arrest me, I insist that you all leave."

After being ushered outside, Judy stopped on the porch and said, "I don't think you realized until now what Mike had done. You haven't done anything wrong, Pat. You could help us."

"I told you, Mike was lying," Pat said, shutting the door in Judy's face.

Slowly, she made her way back to her chair, forgetting about the paint and about her vows not to think about the past.

She put her head in her hands and held on tight, commanding the demons to shut up and leave her in peace.

When she allowed herself, she could remember it as if it were yesterday, the night she lay in her brother's bed in Pittsburgh full of anticipation on the arrival of her first child. She had dreams of their baby bringing her and Mike back together – of the three of them, her little family. Dreams of Mike realizing his responsibilities and gaining maturity through the new life he had created.

She remembered creeping downstairs in the middle of the night to eat the meal her mother had set aside for her. She had to tiptoe past Robert sleeping on the sofa, but as she opened the refrigerator door, she felt a searing pain rip through her belly and heard someone screaming. She remembered Robert standing over her and then she was in the hospital with the bright lights and people bustling around - until the lights went out.

The next thing she knew, Linda was on her lap and they were driving home. She remembered being overcome by a tremendous feeling of loss, even while looking at her beautiful new daughter. She had no idea why. She thought it was because of her father's death and because she had missed his funeral. But as the years went by, the nameless loss deepened and became darker. Every time she looked at Linda, she was reminded of her inability to feel. It was as if the drugs they gave her to numb her pain had also numbed all of her other feelings. Pat realized after she had her second daughter, she and Linda had never bonded as they should have.

Mike was sweet about it at first, told her it was post-partum depression and that everything would work out. But as the months went by and she was still struggling to pull herself out of whatever deep well her mind had fallen into, he got impatient and angry. He once blurted out, "After what I did for you, you should be grateful. Not walking around here all morbid." She had taken it to mean that she should be grateful he had married her.

He really started drinking then, the few jobs he found never lasted long and he was sometimes stone cold drunk when she got home from work, even though he was supposed to be watching the kids. It was the drinking that really tore them apart. She learned to stuff her feelings deep inside her, never knowing when something she said or a look on her face would trigger his rage.

Pat used to think of their life together as a wild coaster ride, but it became increasingly scary and dangerous. She began to think that she didn't know this man anymore.

She had loved Mike her whole life and had sacrificed her family's love for his. And all the while he had been keeping this horrendous secret from her. He hadn't even been man enough to tell her when she went to say her final goodbye. Instead, he had exposed their shame to strangers.

She knew it was true; knew now that she had been a fool. She couldn't believe she hadn't put it together before this. She had purposely and proudly held her head high, but now realized her life had been a sick delusion.

She hadn't previously been able to face it because it was too horrible. Their family name would become linked with Seth McPherson's. None of her children, nor her mother or brother, deserved that.

She had worked all these years to prove that her family was wrong about Mike, cleaning up the messes he left in his wake and covering over his infidelities and weaknesses, just so she could hold her chin up in public. She had raised his children, or so she thought, on her own. No small feat. But this was unfathomable. She couldn't delude herself into thinking these people would just go away and forget. They would dig and prod until the whole ugly truth came out.

What a fool she had been, she thought wearily, as she climbed the stairs to retrieve the sleeping pills her doctor had given her. Mike was right. Some things just couldn't be undone.

~ ~ ~ ~

"That woman is in a world of denial," Judy said to everyone sitting around the dinner table. "You should have seen the look in her eyes when Drew asked her about Georgi's birthmark!"

"Yeah, I thought she was going to come unglued," Les said. "But she pulled herself together and grew even more obstinate."

They had decided to go back home to Pennsylvania, even though Les had the address of one of Pat's daughters. Andrew wanted to think it through and develop some sort of strategy before he had a conversation with any of the other Bigelows, who no doubt had been called and warned not to talk to him.

Les felt there was now enough evidence to open a full scale investigation into the Bigelow family.

Frank and Louise had come over for dinner and Mae had put out a feast they were now digesting, along with the information that had been gathered thus far. Mae called it a celebration, but Andrew was not feeling particularly jubilant. He was sure that he would find Georgi; that all the years of chasing false leads and dashed hopes had led them to her doorstep. But now that it was so close, he was apprehensive about whom he would find; his sweet, beautiful daughter, or a copy of the bitter, angry woman who had raised her.

"Why would a woman like Pat Bigelow defend and pine over a bastard like Mike for all those years," John mused. "I just don't get it."

"Happens all the time," Judy said. "Women begging for love and attention, even if that attention is a punch in the face."

"Seems like a matter of plain old self-worth," Frank said. "Or lack thereof."

They were discussing the merits of opening an official investigation to speed the process of getting answers. Les said that he would then be able to subpoena witnesses.

"But will we be able to keep it out of the public's eye if we do that?" Andrew asked.

"Last thing this family needs is another circus when the papers get a hold of it," Mae grumbled. "The children are having enough problems without adding this to the pot."

"I don't want anyone to know about this except those we choose to tell," Andrew said, making his decision. "There's no telling what kind of emotional state Georgi will be in when we find her, judging by what we've seen and heard already."

Looking at Les and seeing the skepticism on his face, he added, "We *will* find her with or without a subpoena. Robert has promised us that."

"I agree," John said. "He'll help out of self-preservation alone if we can keep this quiet and not let his family get eaten by the media hounds."

Judy was looking at her brother sadly, thinking, *oh my dear Drew. I wish I could prepare you for what you might find.* Instead she said, "I know you're concerned about Georgi and her reaction, but what about you, Drew? What if she doesn't want anything to do with you?"

Frank had been taking it all in and he, too, thought their biggest obstacle was yet to come. "When I was in the Army, we rescued a woman from a POW camp. She had been brainwashed, tortured and abused. She came from good stock though, and the self-confidence she went in with finally pulled her through. It took a long time and a lot of help, but she made it."

"That's what I'm afraid of," Judy said, "that she didn't have the chance to develop that self-confidence."

"Georgi comes from good stock," Mae said. "Her daddy's love and the truth will win her over."

~ ~ ~ ~

Andrew was in the office the next day, trying to catch up on the paperwork that had accumulated in his absence, but more specifically to talk to Robert.

He was hoping that Robert would have more luck talking to his sister, when John came into his office with a frown as deep as Alabama. "What's wrong?" Andrew asked, alarmed at the look on John's face.

"Robert called. His sister took an overdose of pills after we left yesterday. She's dead."

Chapter Nine

"Holy shit! Check out this bathroom! It's bigger than our whole living room at home!"

"It's all very surreal," Linda said to her brother-in-law, Bill, as she looked around the gorgeous hotel suite with her two sisters and their husbands. "Are you sure we have the right one?"

"Go ask him yourself," Bill said. "But you're going to have a hard time moving me now if this is a mistake." He had claimed one of the bedrooms and was already sprawled out on the bed, surfing TV channels.

Linda made her way back to the suite's living room where her Uncle Robert sat with her sister, Mary. *He looks like he's aged ten years since I saw him last*, she thought to herself.

She listened as Mary asked him the question that was on her own tongue, "Why would your boss rent us this suite? It must have cost a fortune."

How could Robert explain it to them? Andrew had come to his house yesterday and they had talked for hours. Both men's emotions were raw from the previous week's events and ranged from anger and accusations, to tears and confessions. Robert felt that he was being implicated in something he knew nothing about, and in turn wanted to blame Andrew for Pat's death. But in truth, he felt guilty for not being there when Andrew had gone to talk to her. He should have gone, he thought.

He and Pat had grown further and further apart since her move to Ohio. It wasn't just the physical distance; the emotional distance seemed to grow every year as well. Pat had become so – hostile, was the only word that came to mind. When had he become the enemy? he wondered. He had learned to keep his mouth shut about Mike long ago. Even so, Pat could sense his concern for her sanity and safety. Lately they had spoken only when it was necessary, and then only about their mother or their children.

In any case, it was too late now to be second guessing how he could have made anything turn out differently. Robert was far too pragmatic to waste his energies on the past when there was so much that needed fixing right now. He and Andrew had spent too many days suspicious of each other's roles and motives in this whole tragedy and the strain was taking its toll at work. Unlike Pat, he had learned a long time ago that just because he wished something, it didn't make it so. His nieces needed him. His family needed him to protect them from this all blowing up on them. He was in the unique position to help both his family and Andrew; to reunite Andrew and Linda and to ease the process for them in whatever way he could.

The thought of what Mike did still shocked the hell out of him. He could almost understand why Pat had such a deadly reaction. But her reaction proved to him that Andrew's suspicions were probably true and she hadn't faced it until the day he showed up on her doorstep.

He couldn't blame Andrew for wanting to find his daughter. If it were him, he thought, he'd be breaking down doors to get to her. But when he expressed as much to Andrew, Andrew had smiled sadly and said that if she were two or three years old, that would be his reaction as well. But now that Georgi was twenty-three years old, he had to be gentle and convince her that he just wanted to open doors for her that she didn't know existed.

"I know you love her too, Robert," he had said, and promised he wouldn't push the truth on her but would help her to accept it. If Robert knew nothing else about Andrew, he knew that Andrew was as good as his word. And so, with reluctance, he had accepted Andrew's offer of this grand hotel suite for Pat's family to stay in while they were in town for the funeral and said to Mary, "He's a generous man . . . and my friend. He knew there wouldn't be enough room at my house for all of you and told me to just accept it with his condolences to the family."

Mary was trying not to cry. Goodness knows she had cried enough in the past three days to fill a bathtub. "That's so sweet of him," she said.

Mary had been the one to find her mother, having gone over to help her paint. It was past noon when she arrived, and she figured her mother would have the room almost done. Mom always got up at the butt-crack of dawn and got busy right away, but Mary couldn't pull herself out of bed early on her day off. So she was surprised when she walked in and found that her mother had barely begun painting. She had pulled up behind her mom's car in the drive, so she knew she was in the house somewhere, but there was no answer when she called out. She stood in the doorway of her mother's bedroom, saw her lying there fully clothed and felt a log of dread drop into her stomach. Something was terribly wrong. Calling her mother's name and beginning to panic when she couldn't get a response, she dialed 911 with shaking hands. A frozen wave of disbelief washed over her, numbing her to the worst moment of her life.

Now in this scrumptious room, she gave up a shiver and said, "Thank you Uncle Robbie, for taking care of everything for us." Her sisters had gotten there soon enough, but they were all too shocked to think straight and had walked around the house wringing their hands until their younger sister, Chris, suggested calling Uncle Robbie.

Chris's husband, Chuck, was rummaging through a basket of pastries and cookies and an assortment of coffee and teas that was on the suite's kitchen counter, pulling out and breaking open a package of chocolate chip cookies. "Wow, your boss went all out here," he said to Robert. "And look, the refrigerator is stocked with drinks and lunch meat and anything else we could possibly want."

"Yeah," Robert smiled. "When Andrew does something, he does it right. You should see the spread he sent to my house."

"Is he coming to the wake tonight?" Chris asked. "I'd like to thank him personally."

Robert looked at Linda, who had yet to say anything. Her glazed eyes said she was trying to take in her surroundings but it just didn't compute. He and Andrew had agreed that they would wait until after the funeral to talk to her. It was so obvious now how different she was from her sisters. Chris and Mary were dark-haired beauties, tall and regal, whereas Linda was a petite blonde and looked more like a fairy. She had Andrew's blue eyes. But it wasn't just her looks that differentiated her from her sisters. Linda was introverted and quiet, compared to Chris and Mary's sociable personalities. He then realized they were both talking to him, "I'm sorry? Oh yes, he'll probably be there tonight."

"You didn't tell him about Mom's ... ah, the cause of death, did you?" Chris asked. "We decided to tell everyone that it was a heart attack. We think it would be better that way."

"Speak for yourself," Linda spoke at last, a bit too hostile, even for her own ears. She lowered her head and her voice and mumbled, "I'm tired of secrets."

In the ensuing silence, Robert took his opportunity to leave. Standing up from the couch, he said, "Well, I'll let you get settled in and ready for the wake. I'll pick you up out front at 6:30 sharp."

Linda went into her room and shut the door. *I have time for a short nap*, she thought. She loved sleep more than anything; loved drifting off into nothingness. But right now, instead of sleep, her mind was boiling a muddled brew. She knew that it wasn't for their mother's benefit they were lying to everyone. None of them could face the look of pity in people's eyes if they told the truth, nor the accusations they felt would be directed toward them - the ones who should have known and stopped her. They were dealing with the guilt, each in their own way, having made an unspoken pact not to discuss it. But it was there, hanging on them like cement coats that couldn't be shed.

While both her sisters had cried rivers, she hadn't shed a tear. *Why can't I cry?* she wondered. She hadn't cried when she heard the news about her father's death either. Was it only a couple of weeks ago? Time had come to a standstill and she felt like she was living in a vacuum of numbness, unable to remember even how they had gotten to Pittsburgh for this funeral. It seemed like a long ago dream. Her sisters and the people around her were like ghosts, fading in and out of her consciousness but never really coming into full form. Even when they spoke directly to her, it sounded hazy and blurred.

She was an orphan now, she thought, chiding herself for feeling like a baby when she was a full grown adult. Yet she had never felt so utterly empty and alone. Like an invisible umbilical cord, or anchor, had been cut, freeing an empty plastic bag to drift about the winds.

Hell, she thought, *I am not going to get all maudlin like Mom.* She was pretty sure that her sisters never had thoughts like: *Why was I born?* She had seen firsthand what those kind of self-pitying thoughts had done to her mother and she would not succumb to them. The only thing she did know was that her mother had given up and she would not – but how was she going to get through the next few days?

~ ~ ~ ~

"What?" Linda asked her sister. She tried to focus on Chris' question.

"Where did all these people come from?" Chris asked again. "Mom didn't know this many people."

"I think most of them are Grandma's friends," Mary said. "Look how old they are." They had agreed that the funeral should be in Pittsburgh for their grandmother's sake. After all, funerals were for the living, not the dead, and their mom didn't have many friends in Cleveland. Mary was crying again and Linda had to leave. She snuck outside to have a cigarette and to get away from all these strangers who kept hugging her and telling her how sorry they were. Standing and smoking outside the back door, she watched a woman about her mom's age approach from the parking lot. She had gray permed hair that looked like an afro, and the biggest pair of glasses Linda had ever seen. They practically covered her whole face.

"Are you one of Pat Bigelow's daughters?" afro lady asked.

"Yes, I'm Linda."

"Hi. My name is Cindy. Well, I guess I would be your Aunt Cindy. I'm your dad's sister."

"Oh. Well. Hi." Linda said. She was racking her brain trying to remember if she even knew he had a sister. "Thank you for coming," she said by rote.

"Yes, well I'm a Bigelow too. I guess it's the least I could do. . ." she trailed off. "Actually," she began again, "I wanted to ask you about my brother. He didn't keep in contact with me, but your mom would write notes every so often. I knew he was sick, but I hadn't heard from your mom for a while so I called the hospital in California and found out he died. Your mom never told me. Was there a funeral?"

"No, Mom had him cremated in California." *Come to think of it*, she thought, *I don't even know if she requested his ashes.* She hadn't talked to her mother again after that morning on the phone. She made a mental note to ask Mary, who was closest to Mom and most likely to know.

"Well I wish she had told me he was dying," Cindy said. "I would have gone to say my goodbyes too."

"What do you mean?" Linda asked. "None of us have talked to him in a long time."

Cindy gave her a puzzled look. "Why, when I called the hospital, they said that your mother had been there the week before he died."

"What? No. She said . . ." Linda trailed off, suddenly feeling dizzy, she stubbed out her cigarette.

"I'm quite sure," the bugged-eyed woman said. But Linda didn't hear what else she was rambling on about because she was trying to replay the tape of their last conversation. Her mother had said she didn't know her father had been sick, that she didn't know where he was until they called to tell her he was dead. She wanted to tell this woman she was crazy, but Linda had a lot of experience in hearing her mother's secrets out of other people's mouths. Nothing ever seemed to add up, and when she used to confront her mother, it just ended up in a fight and more confusion, so Linda had stopped questioning long ago.

Shaking her head to clear it, she asked Cindy, "What did you say?"

"I said they think your mother was the one who gave Mike the gun he used to shoot himself."

Linda had to get away, find somewhere to sit down. *He shot himself?* Finding an empty loveseat in the back of the room, she tried to hide from the prying eyes that seemed to know more about her parents' lives and deaths than she did.

This feeling reminded her of when she was a little girl and her mother had taken them to the beach. She had been playing by herself in knee-deep water close to shore when suddenly, the sand gave out from underneath her and she was caught up in a rip tide. The more she struggled and gasped for air, the more the swirling water pulled her under. She fought and swam as hard as she could but knew it was stronger than she was; that she was going to die right there on the shoreline. It felt like an eternity and her lungs were about to burst when her foot caught hold of a steady piece of ground and she was able to crawl out, coughing and spitting up water. When she looked up, she saw her mother was sitting not even ten feet away, reading a book. When she told her what had just happened, her mother looked at her scornfully and told her not to be so melodramatic.

She wished she could find a foothold now that would enable her to crawl out of this whirlpool of confusion. She looked at her mother lying in her casket and could almost see that same look of disgust on her face, as if she were watching her drowning in her own turmoil and chiding her for it.

"Are you all right?" A man she didn't know sat down beside her on the loveseat. She could feel the concern in his voice and she slid over closer to her end of the couch.

She looked down at her hands in her lap, then around the room for an exit. She had to get out of here without appearing to be too rude.

"Linda?"

His voice was soft, beckoning her to look at him.

She looks like a wild animal I've just backed into a corner, Andrew thought, desperate to take her in his arms and hold her, although he was sure she would run off if he attempted. He knew in his soul that she was Georgi. When she finally turned to him, every ounce of compassion he had in his heart went out to ease the pain and pleading that were so evident in her blue eyes.

"Is there anything I can do to help you?" he asked lamely, feeling helpless and awkward.

"No. But thank you Mr. . . . ."

"Andrew Lexington," he said, and although it took all of his willpower, he got up to give her the space her eyes were pleading for.

She looked back down at her hands. Something about this man was so disturbing, but maybe it was just her state of mind at the moment. He seemed so kind. Too kind. Too familiar. Something about his eyes, like they were seeing inside of her. She felt totally exposed in his gaze. For a crazy split second, while he was sitting there beside her, she had the urge to grab onto him and cry her eyes out. Everything was upside down right now and she was just feeling melodramatic she thought, looking again at her mother.

~ ~ ~ ~

Linda slept late the next morning. Still, she saw with relief that she was the first one up. She tiptoed back into her room and shut her door, grateful for some time alone. Getting her book out and propping herself up in bed, she was thinking that her sisters were probably having a lazy morning with their husbands. She was envious that they had someone to lay in bed and talk with. She and her ex-husband hadn't had that kind of relationship. It was either sex or sleep with him, so it was just as well that she was alone with her book and her uninterrupted thoughts.

Last night when they were having a drink before turning in for the night, she told everyone what the bug-eyed aunt had said. Mary hadn't been shocked at all, even though she said she hadn't known about Mom visiting Dad in California. Mary had her own perspective of their mother that ranged somewhere between her being a star-crossed lover to a romantic martyr, much like all the trashy novels she read. The fact that their mom may have visited him to say goodbye forever and give him a gun to end his terminal suffering, then take her own life less than two weeks later, just reinforced her illusions. *Talk about the melodramatic one*, she thought.

Linda, usually exasperated with Mary's way of looking at life, was now thinking that it was a much simpler way to live than her typical pessimism. Don't they always say that it's all in how you look at things?

That's it: today I'm going to put it all behind me, bury my father and mother and then live my own life.

She had no idea that now their ghosts could invade her mind, like the spirits they were, and speak to her incessantly about their secrets and their suffering.

Hearing people in the kitchen, she got out of bed, already forgetting to don her new attitude and thought, *let's get this day over with.*

Chuck and Chris were making breakfast from the stock of food in the refrigerator, bantering over which one made the best fried eggs.

"We don't have any onions, so my award winning eggs won't be quite as good today," Chuck teased.

Chris wasn't the morning person Chuck was and was still a little grumpy. "Don't you dare tell Andrew that he forgot something, after all he's done for us," she warned.

"Oh my God," Linda said, remembering. "I met him yesterday and I think I was terribly rude."

"What do you mean, rude?" Mary asked. "How could you possibly be rude to that sweet man?"

"I was in a fog and I didn't realize who he was until after he left," Linda said.

Chris and Mary gave each other a look that said, "So what else is new?"

"Did you talk to him?" Linda asked them.

"Oh yes," Mary said. "I've never met anyone so rich who is so incredibly down to earth. It felt like he was family or something."

Linda remembered his genuine concern for her. "I know what you mean, it was almost like he knew me," she said. "I hope he comes to the funeral today so I can apologize."

"It's so sad about his daughter," Mary said.

"What about his daughter?" Linda asked. Chris was nodding her head in agreement.

"Aunt Mary and Aunt Peggy told us yesterday that his daughter was kidnapped when she was just an infant," Chris said. "They never found her, or her body."

"Wow, that is sad," Linda said, having a new appreciation for the empathy he had shown her. "When did this happen?"

"Back when they were teenagers," Mary said, "so it was a long time ago. But he has never stopped looking for her. Isn't that the most heart-breaking story you ever heard?" she asked.

~ ~ ~ ~

I should go to church more often, Linda thought, sitting in the pew for her mother's service. *There's something so comforting about being here*, and for the second time in as many days, she thought that she might cry. But Mary and Chris were doing enough crying for all of them. Their mom used to take them to church all the time when they were young, but as soon as Linda got married and left home, she quit going. *Mom's God was a very hard task master*, she thought. She was afraid to think any more of what her mom's God would do to her for the sin of suicide.

She felt the eyes of the congregation on the back of her head and avoided their pity by looking out the window. *I'm so glad we decided not to go to the gravesite*, she thought. It was a cold and sleeting January day and the thought of months more of this weather brought an oppression that the hymns couldn't lift.

Andrew was standing in the church lobby when they filed out after the service. His eyes lit up when he saw her and she was relieved to see he didn't look angry with her. *Still*, she thought, *I need to go over and apologize to him*. Her mother was a stickler for good manners.

She shook his hand and said, "I didn't get to meet you properly yesterday, Mr. Lexington. I apologize for my rude behavior. I don't know where my head was."

"No need to apologize. Your sorrow is totally understandable and I didn't mean to intrude," Andrew said.

"The hotel suite is very generous of you, thank you," she said.

"My pleasure. I'd like you to meet my family."

She now noticed the people standing around him were staring at her in anticipation of an introduction. The colored lady closest to him looked like she was about to burst with something she wanted to say. "Pleased to meet you, Mae," she said when Andrew had introduced them.

"Oh my child," was all Mae could sputter before giving Linda the biggest, warmest hug she had ever received. Linda was taken a little off guard by her exuberance and stood there mute until Mae released her and looked her up and down like she was doing an inspection.

"And this is my sister, Judy," Andrew said. Judy, too, gave her a hug and told her she was happy to meet her, then introduced her husband and children, who were grinning at her like they were cats who had just swallowed the family canary.

"Are you Georgi?" asked the youngest one, Ali.

"Oh don't pay her any attention," Mae said apologetically, while giving Ali a glare.

"Georgi is my daughter," Andrew said by way of explanation.

"Oh," Linda remembered now about his kidnapped daughter. "I was very sorry to hear about that."

"Yes, well she'd be about your age," Andrew said.

"It's a perfectly understandable question then," she said to Ali, who had grown sullen at the chastising looks she was getting from everyone.

Uncle Robert came up behind them and said, "We're serving lunch in the church basement and we'd be honored to have you and your family join us, Andrew."

Andrew looked at Linda as if to ask for her permission.

What is it about this man's eyes? she thought. It was very disconcerting - they wouldn't let her go. "Please," she said, "we'd love it if you would stay."

Robert led them downstairs, talking a mile a minute. *It's not like him to be so chatty*, Linda thought, but chalked it up to wanting to make a good impression for his boss.

She had hoped to sneak out and skip the lunch, slipping back to the hotel room after the service so she wouldn't have to smile any more at all these people. But there was no chance of that now. She didn't want to be rude to Andrew a second time.

Standing in the buffet line, she was forced to make small talk, which she hated. But Judy was making it easy, asking her questions about her job or a boyfriend and acting like she really wanted to hear her answers.

"Your hair is just like mine," Judy said.

It was true. Linda saw how Judy's hair was a mass of curls and unruliness.

"Does it look like a firecracker went off on your head when you wake up in the morning?" Judy asked.

Linda had to laugh. "Yes!" she said, "That's just what it looks like."

"I think I've tried everything on the market," Judy said, "and do you know what works the best?"

"No, what?" Linda asked. "I've tried everything too but it still does whatever it wants."

"Olive oil," Judy said. "Plain old olive oil, but just a little bit or it will look like you never wash your hair."

John was finishing up in the buffet line and held up a ladle of salad dressing. "I could help you girls out," he said. "Would you like me to anoint your curls with oil?"

Linda giggled like a schoolgirl and Judy gave John a playful punch on the arm. Part of Linda wanted to stay with these people and the other part wanted to run away. She opted for running away and said, "If you'll excuse me, I better go see what my grandmother wants to eat. She's sitting there alone and without lunch. It was nice meeting you." She couldn't bring herself to look at Andrew and the eyes that bore through her.

What is it about him? she wondered, as she walked toward her grandmother. *Is he trying to put the moves on me? That's crazy; he's old enough to be my father.*

When she reached the table, her Aunt Peggy was bringing her grandmother's lunch and Linda sat down next to them, hungry all of a sudden.

"Is Andrew married?" she asked.

"My, no," Aunt Peggy said. "His wife died of a broken heart not long after their baby was kidnapped."

"That's so sad," Linda said, looking over at him. Judy was talking seriously to him about something and he was nodding his head in agreement. It looked intense. "They're just the nicest family."

"That's what Robert says," her grandmother agreed. "He practically idolizes the man, and it's no wonder. Andrew is good to all his employees, but he's particularly taken Robert under his wing and is grooming him to take over part of his business."

"I'm surprised he hasn't gotten married again," Linda said. "That was a long time ago."

"Heck, if I weren't married, I'd certainly have my eye on him!" Aunt Peggy exclaimed. "He's so handsome and so rich, he's the most eligible bachelor in town."

Her grandmother told her Robert said everyone keeps trying to fix him up with dates, but Andrew will have none of it.

"So he's not a playboy?" Linda asked.

Laughing, her grandmother said, "Far from it, according to Robert. He spends all his time either working or looking for his daughter."

"The little girl asked me if I was Georgi," Linda said.

"I imagine they would see their Georgi in just about every woman around your age," said her grandmother. She looked at Linda for a minute and then said, "Come to think of it, you were born on the same day his daughter was kidnapped."

"Are you sure?" Linda asked, feeling a shiver run through her.

"I'm positive," her grandmother said. "It was the same day as your granddaddy's funeral."

Chapter Ten

Linda wished she had more time to talk with her grandmother, but they had been interrupted and then it was time to say their goodbyes and rush to the airport to make their flight back to Cleveland. Now on the plane going home, Linda was thinking about what her grandmother had told her. The coincidence of her birth being the same day as Andrew's daughter's kidnapping was kind of weird, and yet, it had triggered a longing in her. There had never been any stories about the day she was born; stories of which abounded when it came to her sisters. Nor had there been stories of things she had done, cute or otherwise, as a baby. It was a big black hole, and those few words from her grandmother had caused her to again tumble down that rabbit hole of self-pity.

This is stupid, she scolded herself. *You can't bring back the past or re-live it. It's over.*

"When are you going to Florida with the Lexingtons?" Chris, who was sitting beside her on the plane, asked, interrupting her pity party.

"I don't know that I am," Linda said, coming out of her reflection in a crabby mood. Judy had pulled her aside after lunch when they were all saying their goodbyes. She told

Linda she had a proposition for her, and asked if she would consider going with them to help babysit the children when they went to their home in Fort Lauderdale for spring break. They would pay her, of course, and she would have time on her own, too, to do whatever she wanted. Linda hadn't had a vacation in years and had never been to Florida. The idea was intriguing and they were really nice people, but she didn't know if she could spend a whole week at their house without feeling suffocated, as she had these last few days of the funeral. All she could think about was escaping everyone's watchful eyes and getting back home.

"Man, I wish they had asked me," Chris said. "I'd go in a heartbeat."

"They only asked me because I'm single," Linda said, oblivious to any significance there might be to singling her out.

"Still, it's an opportunity of a lifetime," Chris said. "If I were you, I'd go. When do you have to let them know?"

"Judy said she comes to Cleveland all the time for work," Linda replied. "She's going to call me next time she's in town for lunch so we can talk about it."

"I can't even imagine getting on a plane where it's snowing and freezing and getting off in a place where it's sunny and warm," Chris said wistfully. "It would be like landing in another world or something."

Another world is right, Linda thought. Hanging around the Lexingtons for a week would feel like she was living in a whole different world for sure.

~ ~ ~ ~

Letting herself into her apartment later, she wondered why she had been so anxious to get home. She was again feeling like that empty plastic bag drifting in the wind. She thought about calling her girlfriend and going out, but she was too tired. Instead, she climbed into bed and pulled the covers up over her head, wishing she could make the world go away. The thought of going to work the next day made her sick to her stomach.

Her mother's death and subsequent funeral had allowed her to forget, but the shame now surged back, threatening to drown her. She had been so flattered when Tom had asked her out. He was the most popular guy in the gang who regularly went out to happy hour after work. They had gone on their "date," which turned out to be grabbing some beers from the 7 Eleven and going to his apartment. They were barely inside when he began grabbing at her clothes and forcing himself on her. In reply to her protests at his abrupt coldness afterwards, he jeered, "What did you expect?"

She was angrier at herself than at him. Her mom had ranted incessantly that men were out for one thing only, but Linda hadn't wanted to believe her. She should have known better.

It confused and hurt her why someone she considered a friend would treat her that way. Worse, the next day at work, he had bragged to everyone that she had begged him for it and that she was a tramp.

She was humiliated! *Well*, she thought, *if pride goeth before a fall, as her grandmother always said, then I'm safe because I have no pride left.* She would just go in tomorrow and do her job, ignoring them all.

The phone rang and she ignored it too.

~ ~ ~ ~

"I'm tired of one night stands," Linda said to her best friend, Jill. "I wish I could just meet someone and quit doing this." She looked around at the crowded bar and watched the guys checking out the girls while the girls pretended they didn't notice.

"Like that's not why we're here," Jill said. "I thought that was the point in us getting all dolled up. We have to put ourselves out there. These guys aren't going to come knocking at our door."

This was an old argument. It seemed like they had this conversation every time they went out.

"Yeah, but half of these guys are married, and the other half are either dorks or guys just looking for a little action tonight," Linda said.

"And what's so wrong with a little action?" Jill snickered. "It's better than no action, isn't it? You want we should go to some church group to meet guys?" she snorted. "They're *all* dorks there."

"Oh, I don't know," Linda said. "Did you ever think that maybe there's something else we should be doing with our lives?"

"Like what?" Jill demanded. "Like take a pottery class or something?" she snorted again, this time shooting a swig of beer out her nose.

"Come on, lighten up Lin," she said, regaining her composure. "I know you just buried your mom and all, but you've been a real downer lately."

"Sorry," Linda said sheepishly. "It's just that I feel . . . different somehow."

"You're just feeling your mortality," Jill said philosophically. "But we're young and hell, the best looking girls in this place, if I do say so myself. If you don't put a smile on your face soon, you'll end up like that old lady sitting down there at the end of the bar. Look at her, she's got to be pushing fifty and how pathetic is that?"

"Gee, thanks for the pep talk," Linda said sourly.

"Oh come on, we're all looking for love. The guys, too, whether they know it or not. We've just got to show them how fabulous we are."

"Like we're on display in the Macy's window," Linda muttered. Louder, she said, "Don't you ever feel like there's some other purpose to it all?"

Laughing, Jill said, "What greater purpose is there than love? Come on, let's dance. I love this song."

"You go," Linda said. "I don't feel like dancing." She lit another cigarette and watched Jill make her way through the crowd to the dance floor. She had hoped that coming out tonight would shake off the morbid mood she'd been in, but for some convoluted reason, being here was magnifying it.

Work today had been a living hell. She thought she could just ignore the stares and the gossip, which were bad enough, but worse still was the look on Tony's face when he asked her if it was true. Instead of his usual puppy-dog adoration, she was feeling his bitter disappointment. She had fallen off the pedestal he had put her on. The pedestal, and the image he had of her, shattered like the fragile glass it was made of and there was no putting it back together. She had no explanation nor excuse for what she had done.

Tony had asked her out countless times and she always used the work ethics excuse. The truth was, his feelings, which he wore on his sleeve, scared her too much. But Tom, who had never given her the time of day, offhandedly asked her out and she had run after him like a puppy dog wagging its tail.

Tom had instigated the whole mess and yet she was the one abandoned. As usual for a Friday, the whole group was going out after work, but there was no, "You coming, Linda?" *It just wasn't fair*, she thought.

So she called Jill and here she was, still unable to shake off the look of aggrieved disappointment in Tony's eyes, which was worse than anything her mother ever said with regard to her being a whore. Her mother didn't have any justification, at least, until Linda had finally given it to her. But Tony's revulsion made everything her mother said about her true.

You stupid, stupid girl, she thought.

"Did you know it's a crime for a beautiful woman to be sitting alone?"

Linda looked up at the man with the deep velvet voice. He was neatly dressed and smelled of some expensive aftershave. His smile invited her to smile back.

"Can I buy you a drink?" he was already signaling the bartender and sitting down in the chair Jill had vacated.

She had been nursing her beer, thinking she would go home and crawl under the covers. She and Jill drove separately so they wouldn't have to depend on each other for a ride home. Which was a good thing, since Jill seemed to have disappeared. *Maybe one drink*, she thought, melting into his dark brown eyes.

"Thank you," she said. "But I'm warning you, I've had a hell of a day and I've already run my girlfriend off with my foul mood."

He laughed, not at all dissuaded. "Then you really do need a drink. My name is Jake, by the way."

"Linda," she responded in kind, as the bartender set down their beers.

"What was so terrible about your day, Linda?" he asked, fixing his fascinating eyes on her as if he had all night to listen to her answer. They were drawing her under their spell, while simultaneously casting out her twin demons of shame and loneliness.

"Just an argument at work," she downplayed. "What brings you out on this cold winter night?"

"Looking for the girl of my dreams," he laughed in a way that felt like they were sharing the same joke.

"Are you married, Jake?" Suddenly she cared whether he had someone waiting for him to come home tonight.

"I was," he said sadly. "But that's over. What about you?"

"Me too," she said.

"Divorce is the pits," he said. "I really liked being married, being a part of a couple. It wasn't my idea to get divorced, but here I am. Have you thought about getting married again?"

She laughed. "I don't think I could ever trust someone enough," she said truthfully.

"You've got to trust somebody sometime." His smile was saying she could entrust all her secrets to him. "You've got to put the past behind you. Life goes on and, besides, I always land on my feet," he said confidently.

She liked his self-assured manner, the way he had bounced back from a traumatic experience and was looking toward the future.

"How do you just put it behind you like that?" she asked, thinking not only of her failed marriage, but of the more recent debacle with Tom, which she knew would haunt her forever.

"Easy," he said. "It's over. You can't get to where you're going by looking behind you."

"And where are you going, Jake?" she asked.

"Wherever you are," he smiled.

Corny. But cute, she decided. She loved the way she saw herself reflected in his eyes, someone desirable and worthy of all his attention. She wanted to be that woman he saw and share in his confidence of a bright future.

"Then why don't you follow me back to my place?" she asked.

~ ~ ~ ~

"Are you coming over for dinner tonight?" Chris asked through the phone. It had become Linda's custom to spend

Saturday nights with Chris and Chuck, watching old movies and trying not to mourn the fact that she didn't have a date.

"You're not going to believe this, but I've got a date tonight."

"With who?" Chris asked, excited.

"With the most perfect man in the world, that's who," Linda said dreamily, thinking about Jake and the morning they had spent together lounging in her bed. He was everything she had ever dreamed of in a man; sharing and talkative and funny, making her laugh so hard she accidently farted, which made them both howl hilariously.

"I met him last night," she explained to her sister, "and he's taking me out to dinner tonight."

"Wow, two nights in a row? What happened to 'Miss-Cynical-About-Men'?"

"I think those days are finally over," she said. "He's really nice, Chris. And he really likes me. In fact, he just ran home to get some clothes and he's coming right back. I've got a lot of stuff I have to do in the meantime, so I'll call you Monday, okay?"

~ ~ ~ ~

"How can you be so sure?" Linda asked Jake a week later when he told her that he loved her. "I mean, you don't really know me."

"I know you enough to know that I love you," he said. "I know what I want and you're what I want."

Linda wanted to lean on Jake's confidence, it made her feel secure. Besides, she had made a conscious decision to trust him and not be so pessimistic. She had always scoffed at the idea of love at first sight, but Jake was proving that it could happen – to her! Just a week ago she was jaded and cynical about finding a man who would love her and want to be with her. Yet, here she was, sitting across from the man who had rescued her from her loneliness. *Why not?* she thought, *I'm just as good as anyone else.*

"I love you too," she said.

"You're so sweet and innocent, I will always to take care of you," Jake promised.

Jake's all-encompassing arms were a safe haven. He made her happy she wasn't at the mercy of the Toms of the world anymore. While in his arms, the demons that made her feel she was unlovable and exploitable were unable to get to her.

For the rest of the evening and far into the night they made plans for the future and all they would do together. *Jake was so right*, she thought. This is so much better than all the introspection she had been engaged in, especially now that she actually had a future to think about. She felt giddy and light without the old ghosts. She allowed herself to get swept away on the surge of love and attention Jake was lavishing on her. So what if it had happened fast? That's the way life was, one day was dark and dreary and the next day sunny.

"You are the perfect man," Linda said. "You can even cook." Jake was making her a late brunch the next day when the phone rang. Probably Chris, she thought.

"Hi Linda, this is Judy." An awkward silence ensued, so she added, "Judy Lexington?"

"Oh, hi," Linda said, recovering from her temporary lapse of memory.

"I hope I didn't catch you at a bad time," Judy said, "but I was wondering if you were free for dinner tomorrow. I'm going to be in town. Actually, Andrew and I will both be in town, and we'd love to take you to dinner."

"Oh," Linda said lamely. Jake had talked about coming over tomorrow after work and she was hesitant to make plans. Besides, what was she going to talk about for a whole evening? Oh yes, Florida. For sure she wouldn't be going with them now that she'd met Jake.

"Well, I've already made plans for tomorrow night," she said. "I'm sorry."

"It's short notice, I know," Judy said, apologizing. "How about lunch? Would that work?"

That's only an hour. I'll just tell them I can't go to Florida and that will be that. "Sure," she said, "where should I meet you?"

They arranged to meet at the New York Spaghetti House on Ninth Street at noon and Linda was flattered by the excitement she caught in Judy's voice. *She's such a nice lady*, she thought, hanging up the phone.

"Who was that?" Jake asked.

"A really nice lady I met at my mother's funeral. She and her brother are going to be in town and want to take me to lunch tomorrow."

"Why is her brother coming?" Jake asked, suddenly on the alert.

"Oh, I don't know," Linda said, blushing at his implication. "He's old enough to be my father, Jake!"

"Don't be naïve, Linda. Men that age just love innocent young women like you."

"Why do you keep saying I'm so innocent?" Linda asked, feeling as though she had been reprimanded. "I've been married and I've dated a lot. Besides, he really is just a sweet older man."

"You want to believe that, Linda. You don't know men," Jake said.

Linda tried to explain, "His daughter was kidnapped and she would be about my age, so maybe he thinks I'm like her or something. Besides, it's just a lunch." She didn't dare tell Jake that they wanted her to go to Florida with them. As much as he was protesting this lunch, she couldn't imagine what he would say about her spending a whole week with them!

"I feel very protective of you," Jake explained defensively. "I just love you so much and I don't want to lose you," he pouted.

"No way you're going to lose me," Linda purred, putting her arms around his waist from behind as he continued to turn the sausages in the frying pan. "Are we having our first argument?" She wanted to lighten the sullen mood that had appeared like a black cloud over his head. When he didn't acknowledge her hug or her words, she stepped back and asked, "Jake?"

He looked at her then, curiously, as if seeing her for the first time. The coolness in his eyes blew through her like a breeze and made her shudder involuntarily. She tried to think what she had said or done to cause him to be so angry with her. He was jealous of Andrew, she realized. Maybe he was right and Andrew had an ulterior motive. Hadn't she thought that at the funeral herself? Maybe she should call Judy back and cancel lunch if it was going to upset him so much. After all, he was much more important to her than the Lexingtons, whom she might never see again anyway.

"Do you want me to cancel the lunch tomorrow? Because I will if it's going to upset you so much."

The love in his eyes returned as quickly as it had evaporated a moment ago and he was smiling again. She was grateful the ugly cloud had dissipated.

"I trust you," he said. "I just don't trust other men with you. Maybe I'm being over-protective, but ...."

He trailed off as she kissed him. "No other man could love me the way you do," she whispered.

"Then let me prove it to you," he said, turning off the stove and sweeping her up in his arms.

Chapter Eleven

"Good morning." Linda was smiling and greeting everyone at work as though the last month had never happened. It didn't matter that they were staring back as if she had suddenly grown a second nose. It wasn't just a brand new week. It was a whole new life. Jake loved her and that made all the difference. She didn't care what they thought about her anymore. Let them talk.

She called Chris to share her excitement. Chris was laughing at Linda's repetitive proclamations of the wonders of Jake and saying she had never heard Linda sound so happy. If Chris had any reservations about their hasty declarations of love, she wouldn't have voiced them while Linda was flying on cloud nine. It was just too rare and heart-warming to hear Linda talking a mile a minute with so much happiness in her voice.

"When am I going to meet Mr. Wonderful?" Chris asked. "Do you want to bring him over for dinner?"

"Sure, I'll ask him. Oh, and geez, I nearly forgot - Judy Lexington called me yesterday and invited me to lunch with her and Andrew today." Linda hadn't called her back to cancel and was stabbed with a dart of remorse. She couldn't very well stand her up at this late notice. Besides, at the very least, she should tell her in person she wouldn't be going to Florida. Jake hadn't actually asked her to cancel and she hadn't exactly promised to either. He said he trusted her and she knew that her intentions were totally honorable. Whatever intentions Andrew may have were his own problem and didn't affect her or Jake.

"I bet this means that you won't be going to Florida with them now," Chris said, reading her thoughts.

"There's no way I could leave Jake for a whole week. Besides, I think he's jealous of Andrew."

"Andrew?" Chris shrieked. "Why?"

"Probably just because he doesn't know him," Linda said, feeling like she wanted to change the subject. She heard someone call her name and looked up to see the receptionist standing in front of her desk with a huge bouquet of red roses. There had to be at least two dozen roses in the vase! "Oh my gosh!" she screamed into the phone. "No one has ever sent me flowers before!"

"Read the card," Chris shouted.

Linda could only read a word at a time, between sobs, she said, "Thank you. .for. . the. . best. . week. .of. .my. .life," but couldn't get out the 'Love, Jake' because she was crying too hard.

"Ahhhhh," Chris sighed. "He sounds so sweet."

~ ~ ~ ~

Linda was being pushed by a wind tunnel up Ninth Street from the lake and trying not to slip on the icy sidewalk. She felt all the street signs were pointing fingers at her, reprimanding her for not canceling this lunch . . . until she opened the wooden door to the restaurant and was embraced in a warm hug of welcome by the aromatic balm of garlic and tomato sauce. The waiters in this quaint Italian family restaurant appeared to have been brought over from the old country the day before yesterday; older gentlemen who didn't speak much English, but whose wide grins and nodding heads made you feel as welcome as if you were in their home for dinner. It was a small place and she saw that Judy and Andrew were already seated by the window. She returned their wave and told the host that she would join them at their table. With a flourish, he escorted her, waiting patiently, her chair pulled out, while both Judy and Andrew gave her hugs of greeting. "I just love it here," she said, shrugging out of her heavy coat. "Good choice, Judy."

"This is a great place," Andrew agreed. "So good to see you again."

Andrew's blue eyes probed Linda with such intensity, she had to look down at the red and white checkered tablecloth, hoping that her blushed face blended in with it like a

Chameleon blended into its surroundings. *Oh, why hadn't Judy come alone?* she thought. *It would have been so much easier.*

Judy seemed to sense that Andrew made her uncomfortable. She tried to make conversation by saying, "My office is over on Huron so I come here whenever I get the chance."

"I saw that on the business card you gave me," Linda said. "How often do you come to Cleveland?"

"Depending on the circumstances, sometimes several times a month," Judy said.

The waiter came to take their orders. Linda was dying for a drink to calm her nerves, but followed the lead of her hosts and ordered a Coke.

When the waiter had gone, Judy asked, "So what's new with you, Linda? You look much happier than you did at the funeral, of course, but has someone else put that glow on your face?" There was a wicked gleam in her eyes.

Judy was smiling at her. *Was she that transparent?* She blushed again and said, "Well, I met a wonderful man. His name is Jake and he just sent me two dozen roses!" she gushed.

Judy laughed. "I *knew* it!"

Linda glanced through her eyelashes at Andrew. He was smiling too, as if he were sharing her happiness, which disarmed her. Maybe she and Jake had been wrong about Andrew's intentions after all. She was beginning to feel more comfortable, and a hint of regret at not being able to spend a week with them in Florida seeped in to weaken her resolve.

Before she could change her mind, she blurted out, "That's why I wanted to tell you in person that I can't go on vacation with you. I can't leave for a whole week. I'm sorry."

By the silence that followed, she figured she had just ruined this lunch, but oh well, she had to do it.

Andrew totally surprised her, however, by saying, "Why don't you and Jake both come?"

"What?" Had she heard him right?

"Sure," he continued. "I...we...would really like you to come and I'd like to meet Jake. Why don't you talk to him and you can let us know later. In the meantime, let's just enjoy our lunch."

"That's so kind of you," she gushed.

Their food was placed in front of them and they busied themselves with napkins and utensils. Grateful for the interlude, she wondered what Jake would say to Andrew's offer. She realized she was hoping he would agree. She had to keep reminding herself that Judy and Andrew were practically strangers, but now that she was with them again, she remembered how comfortable and familiar they felt.

"I have to tell you, though," Andrew said eventually, "that the reason I came with Judy today was to make sure you wouldn't later think that I lured you to Florida under false pretenses."

"I don't understand," Linda said, looking at his now-serious face.

"You know that my daughter was kidnapped 23 years ago." Andrew said.

"Yes. My grandmother said that I was born on the day that your daughter was taken." Linda couldn't help but be relieved that this was about his daughter and not the ignoble "pretenses" that Jake had so direly predicted. She let herself breathe again and smiled, signaling Andrew to continue.

"I'm just asking you to hear me out," he said.

Linda remembered Judy's little girl asking her if she was Andrew's daughter. "Why? Do you think I'm your daughter?" she asked in amusement.

"Yes, I believe that you are," Andrew said.

Linda searched his face. He was totally serious.

Judy broke the stare-down by asking, "Do you realize how much you look like Andrew? And me too, for that matter?"

Linda had been thinking the same thing as she stared into Andrew's eyes. She could understand why they would think this. "Do you believe this too?" she asked Judy, understanding now why they were taking so much interest in her. It wasn't because of *her*, but because they thought she was someone else.

"I do," Judy said, "and not just because of the physical similarities, but also because of the evidence."

"What evidence?" Linda was not sure whether she was hurt or angry or both. "You mean the coincidence that I was born on the same day?" she snapped.

"No," Andrew said. "Mike Bigelow asked me to go to California to talk to him before he died."

"You talked to my father?" Linda was incredulous.

"He told me that he took you out of my house to replace the stillborn baby Patricia had borne that same day."

Time froze. The waiters stopped in mid-stride. Diners froze with forks half way to their mouths. The silence was deadening. The only thing Linda heard was her heart pounding in her ears.

After what seemed like an eternity, the room viciously burst back into life and the noise of dishes clanging and people talking all at once made Linda flinch. She saw Andrew's mouth moving, but couldn't make out what he was saying above the din of the restaurant. She saw the concern on Judy's face and the intensity of Andrew's convictions and abruptly couldn't look at them anymore.

"You're crazy. I have to go," she said, standing up, but staggering from the weight on her legs, which were as limp as the noodles left untouched on her plate.

Andrew jumped up to take hold of her arm and steady her.

Linda stared at his hand on her arm as if she had just grown another appendage.

Judy rose to come around the table. She tried and put her arms around Linda, but Linda pushed her away. In her tangled web of emotions, she spat out, "I've got to go," adding more drama to the scene she was creating in the restaurant.

"Let us drive you somewhere, at least," Judy said.

Linda was staring at the floor and shaking her head.

Andrew took hold of her arm again to deposit an envelope in her hand.

Linda looked at the envelope and then up at him in question. To her surprise, silent tears were streaming down his face as she stood stiff, reluctantly allowing him to give her a hug.

As he held her, he whispered in her ear, "You're going to have a lot of questions later. I'll stay in town for a few days; the number is in that letter. I want to answer all of your questions whenever and wherever you'd like, so call me when you're ready, okay?"

Linda stumbled back down Ninth Street, the bitter wind blowing at her face and freezing her tears. She was blindly headed back to her office, but once she got close and realized what she was doing, she knew she couldn't go back to work. All she wanted was to go home to her warm bed. *Why were these people messing with her mind? They're obviously wrong about her father. I can't think about it*, she decided, as she boarded a bus for home.

Chapter Twelve

Andrew paced his hotel suite. "Don't say 'I told you so,'" he said to Judy, who was sitting in a wing chair by the window, looking out at the tops of hooded heads focused on trying to make their way across the icy square.

"I can't say that," she said, turning to look at Andrew, "What choice did you have?"

"I should have asked Chris or Mary to come with her. I just hate that she's alone right now."

"We don't know that she's alone," Judy said. "She may have called one of her sisters or her boyfriend."

"Maybe I'll call Chris or Mary and have them go check up on her," Andrew said.

"Are you thinking that she might do something as drastic as Pat? Because I don't think she will."

"No," Andrew said. "I'm just feeling the pain of her world being turned upside down."

Judy looked at him sympathetically. "I know. Me too. She's a strong girl though, she'll come through this. I just hate to see you waiting here for her to call. What if she doesn't?"

"What if she does?" Andrew asked. "I have to be here."

"All right, there's no talking you out of it, but I have to get back home," she said, reluctantly getting up from her chair. "I wish I could stay and keep you company."

Andrew gave her a hug. "Don't you worry, I've got lots of paperwork to keep me company."

~ ~ ~ ~

Linda unplugged her phone, took a sleeping pill and was now dreaming that her mother was standing in their old dining room, pounding on the door to the basement and calling out to her father to put the gun down and come upstairs. It was the middle of the night and Linda was standing in the corner watching, but her mother was crying violently and too intent on pleading with her father to realize Linda was there. She kept saying, "Please don't do this. We'll work it out," as she pounded on the locked door.

She woke up in a haze, realizing that the pounding was coming from her own apartment door. Getting up and staggering toward the noise, she mumbled, "Who is it?"

"It's me," Jake said. "Open the door, I've been worried sick about you."

She opened the door and said, "Oh Jake, I'm so happy to see you," crying with the relief of being in the safety of his strong arms again.

"What's wrong, sweetie?" he asked. They were inside her apartment and he sat her down on a chair. "I tried calling you at work and at home and when you didn't answer I got worried."

Still crying, Linda said, "I'm sorry, Jake. Did I tell you that my father shot himself? And my mother killed herself with pills and it's all my fault!"

He took her in his arms again and said, "Now how is that all your fault, Linda?"

Sobbing, "I...don't...know."

"Come on, honey, don't cry. I'm sure it wasn't your fault. It's not good for you to hole yourself up in your apartment like this. Why don't you get dressed and we'll go out and get a couple of drinks and something to eat? That will make you feel better."

"Okay," she sniffed. "I'm sorry."

~ ~ ~ ~

They went to a little hole-in-the-wall place by Linda's apartment because she didn't feel like getting dressed up. Jake had been right. Getting out and listening to some music and sipping a drink was making her feel better and she told him so.

"You've got to chase those blues away, Linda. You can't let yourself wallow in the past. Now let me see that smile of yours."

She smiled at him and said, "What would I do without you, Jake?"

"So did you get the flowers I sent you, or did you think they were from some other guy?" Jake asked.

"Oh my gosh! How rude of me. Of course I knew they were from you," she giggled. "They're beautiful. Thank you!"

"I thought that maybe you would have called to tell me you got them," Jake said, irritation edging his voice. "Then when I couldn't get a hold of you, I got worried that something had happened."

"I'm so sorry, Jake," she said. "I got them right before lunch and then….well, I got upset and went home and unplugged the phone."

"Why? What happened?"

"I met Judy and Andrew," she glanced at Jake, whose eyes were narrowing, so she hurried on, "just because I couldn't very well stand them up, and Andrew said he talked to my father before he died…."

"I knew this was about Andrew," Jake interrupted. "He's the reason you wouldn't even call to thank me and why you just disappeared," Jake said.

"It's not what you think," Linda said. "He thinks I'm his daughter."

"Of course he's going to say that," Jake snapped. "Are you so gullible that you'll fall for that bullshit?"

Linda looked at him like she had just been slapped.

"I'm sorry, sweetie," Jake said quickly, realizing he had gone too far. "It's just that you're so innocent, you think guys are nice. I just want to protect you. I love you, honey. I was worried sick about you today."

"I should have called you, I'm sorry. I didn't mean to worry you." Linda wanted to tell him that she was a big girl and could take care of herself, but she was beginning to wonder about the truth of that statement. Besides, she had briefly glimpsed their relationship teetering on a precipice, about to fall over and shatter. "I guess I'm just not used to someone caring about me so much," she said, relieved to see his face brighten.

"I'll always take care of you," Jake said. "I just want what's best for you and for us, so let's forget about all that crap that happened in the past and about Andrew and his pitiful story and just enjoy our evening, okay?"

"Okay," she said weakly. She didn't want to ruin their time together by talking about her confused feelings. *Plenty of time to sort it out later when she was alone and could think,* she decided.

Jake had returned to his normal, chatty self and she listened as he talked about his day at work. He sold kitchen appliances at Sears and when things were slow in the store, the guys had a tendency to play practical jokes on each other. He wanted to make her laugh, so he told her how someone had once placed a dead mouse on a plate and put it into one of the showroom refrigerators.

"So this family comes into the store," Jake said, "and Luke swings open the door to the refrigerator and the woman screams! You should have seen Luke's face when he looked in and saw the mouse. It was hysterical!"

"Linda? What's the matter?" She was looking at him with her mouth formed in an "O."

"Nothing," she shook her head. "I guess I just don't see how that's funny."

"You're in a foul mood tonight," Jake said, disgusted. "I was trying to lighten things up but you can't even take a joke."

"I'm sorry," she said for the umpteenth time that night. "Maybe I should just go home, I'm not feeling very good."

"Whatever you want," Jake said, signaling the waitress for their check.

~ ~ ~ ~

When they pulled into her parking lot, Linda saw her sister, Mary, huddled in her car trying to stay warm. Jake stopped the car and she jumped out to run over and knock on Mary's window, startling her from her doze. Linda saw that Chris was also in the car. She was afraid of the reason both of them would be sitting out here waiting for her. *Who died now*, was all she could think. "What are you doing here?" Linda yelled through the window.

Getting out of the car, Mary said, "Andrew called. He's worried about you."

In a panic, Linda whispered, "Don't say anything to Jake, I'll explain later." Jake had locked his car and was walking over to them. "Jake, these are my sisters, Mary and Chris."

"What brings you girls out on this frigid night?" Jake asked, shaking their gloved hands.

"Linda unplugs her phone and no one can get a hold of her," Mary said, "so we had to drop by instead. Sorry to mess up your date."

Jake gave Linda a question mark look, silently asking if she was going to tell them to go home. When he saw the pleading in her eyes, he said, "Well, good luck talking to her tonight. I haven't had much success." With that, he turned and walked back to his car.

"Jake?" Linda called.

"Yes?" Jake turned to look, frost coming out of his mouth with the word. His eyes were just as icy.

"I'm sorry," she said weakly.

"Good night, Linda," he said, and turned again toward his car.

Linda watched him go as Chris yanked on her arm, "Come on, let's go in where it's warm."

"Wow, we really made him mad," Mary exclaimed as they climbed the stairs to Linda's apartment.

"It wasn't you," Linda said. "We were having a bad night. Do you want some coffee?"

Mary turned up the heat in Linda's apartment and came into the kitchen to sit down. "Anything hot sounds great."

"Speaking of hot," Chris said, "you're right, Linda. Jake is hot."

Laughing, Linda said, "You mean mad-hot or cool-hot?"

"Both," Chris said. "What were you two fighting about?"

"Andrew. That's why I didn't want you to mention his name. He thinks Andrew is putting the moves on me and using the story about his daughter as a pick-up line."

"He doesn't even know Andrew," Mary said. "If he knew him, he wouldn't think that."

"I know," Linda said sadly, setting the coffee cups on the kitchen table and sitting down with her sisters. "But it's like he's got his mind made up about him."

"He's still jealous of Andrew even after you told him what Andrew said to you today?" Chris asked.

"So he told you?"

"Yes," Mary said. "He called me because he was concerned about you being alone. He told me about what Dad said and I have to say I'm still in shock! I mean, it's so hard to believe!"

"Why didn't you call us?" Chris asked.

"I didn't want to think about it," Linda said. "I don't really believe it. Dad couldn't have done that. Could he?"

"I don't know," Mary said, twirling her spoon in her coffee cup, lost in thought. "Remember the time he stole a Cadillac, parked it in front of the house and told us it was an Easter present?"

"No," Linda said.

"I do," Chris said. "He was playing like it was an Easter egg hunt and then pulled the curtains back to show us the car. The cops came later and arrested him. Mom said he just borrowed it, but the cops wouldn't have arrested him if he had borrowed it from somebody."

"Well a car is a little different than stealing a baby," Linda said. "Even if he did, how would he have gotten away with it all these years? Wouldn't Mom know?"

"Andrew said that she didn't," Mary said. "If she suspected at all, she didn't know for sure until he went to talk to her."

"He talked to Mom, too?" Linda asked incredulously.

"Yes," Mary said sadly. "He was there that day she . . . and then I remembered that your birth certificate had been lying on the dining room table. I didn't think anything of it at the time, I just put it away."

"She must have just realized what happened," Chris said.

"I knew it was my fault," Linda said softly.

"How could it be your fault, Linda?" Chris asked. "It's nobody's fault but her own. You know how she was always covering up for Dad and acting like he could do no wrong."

"She loved him," Mary said defensively. "How tragic it must have been to realize he lied to her about her own child."

"If that's true, it's no wonder she hated me," Linda said.

"She didn't hate you," Mary said, always their mother's defender.

"She treated me differently than she treated you two."

"I always thought it was because you were the oldest - that she was harder on you because of that," Chris said. "But this puts a whole new light on things."

"I'm not saying it's true," Linda quickly explained. "I have a birth certificate that says I'm their daughter."

"Yeah, and the freaky thing is that Andrew has a death certificate with your name on it for same day," Mary said.

Linda shuddered. She got up and poured some whiskey into her coffee, offering the bottle to her sisters. Chris poured some into her own cup, but Mary declined.

"So who *am* I?" Linda asked bitterly. "Am I Linda, or am I Andrew's daughter or am I dead?" She lit a cigarette. Her throat was raw, her head hurt.

"All I know," Chris said, "is that you're still our sister, whether your name is Bigelow or Lexington."

Linda looked at her gratefully. "Thanks," she said. "But I don't believe it. I don't know what to believe."

"Just think," Mary chirped, "if you're a Lexington, you're rich!"

They all laughed at that. "Like Cinderella!" she continued, "only better."

"That makes us sound like we're her evil step sisters," Chris chided, making them all laugh louder.

"Wait," Linda sobered. "We're getting ahead of ourselves. This has to be some freak coincidence or a huge mistake."

"We should go talk to Andrew tomorrow," Mary said. "He said he was staying in town in order to answer our questions."

"That's right, he did," Linda said, getting up to retrieve her purse. "He gave me a letter."

"Read it!" Mary demanded.

"Here it is," she said, as she took the pages out of the envelope and unfolded them.

My dear Linda:

I know you don't yet believe that you're my daughter, Georgi, and I'm sorry that this comes as such a shock to you. There's just no other way of telling you all that I've discovered without causing you great pain and confusion. I want so much to talk to you about it and try to answer your questions.

For now, though, let me give you my own perspective. On the day you were born, I paced the hospital corridor, as anxious and nervous as any new father. My dear wife, Marie, your mother, was a fragile woman. Light as the breeze and just as pure. I was worried for her throughout her pregnancy and worried for you. I used to talk to you through her stomach wall and tell you that you had to be strong for her and be born healthy. Now I'm asking you, through a letter, to be strong...

Linda had to stop reading, choking up.

"Would you like me to continue?" Mary asked, anxious to hear the rest of the letter.

Linda shook her head and cleared her throat.

...to be strong and open your heart and mind to the truth. A simple blood test will reveal the truth.

The day you were born, I wasn't allowed to see you right away. You were so tiny. They put you in an incubator and it was several hours before they would let me go to the nursery. When I walked to the glass window separating me from you, I saw rows and rows of babies in their cribs. You were lying there with your eyes wide open. We saw each other at the same time and shared a moment that was burned into my soul forever. I will never forget the feeling of recognition that passed between us. It felt like I had known you forever and was seeing you again after a long absence.

"Ohhh," Chris and Mary said in unison. Linda stared at those lines remembering what Andrew's burning stares felt like.

"That's so sweet," Mary said.

"Keep reading," Chris said.

Clearing her throat again, she continued.

Of course you now know that it was no accident I was at the funeral. I recognized you the minute I looked into your eyes again. I think that I would have known you if we had passed on the street among strangers. But there you were, sitting on that loveseat in the corner, and my heart knew I had found you.

"How could he keep quiet and not blurt it out?" Chris asked.

"Keep going!" Mary yelled.

I knew that you wouldn't believe me, so rather than cause you more confusion at a time so devastating, I decided to wait until I could talk to you in person. But as you read this now, you'll know that I didn't get a chance to tell you everything I wanted to tell you. As I put myself mentally in your shoes, I may have reacted the same way.

"What a sensitive man!" Mary exclaimed.

Linda continued.

As I said before, I'd like to explain to you in person what facts I've discovered. But for now, let me just tell you

*something so that you will be able to know for yourself that I'm
not making all of this up. My daughter Georgi has a birthmark
on her left buttocks....*

The three of them gasped in concert.

"Your birthmark!" Chris shouted.

"It's true!" Mary said. "It's really true!"

Chris and Mary had always teased her about her
birthmark, saying it was from all the spankings she got as a kid.
Linda had always been embarrassed by it and was glad it was
in a private place. She continued, slowly reading the rest of the
letter.

*...that looks like an imprint of a hand. Mae says that's
God's handprint and the thought has always given me faith
that I would find you. Unbeknownst to you, I have been
searching for you your whole life. I've thought about you
every single day. I've wondered about when you took your first
step or what your first words might be. You've turned into a
beautiful woman, just as I had imagined. You look so much
like your mother, it takes my breath away.*

*I know that you have a lifetime of memories to support
your belief of who you are and I know that we can't re-live our
lives or change what's happened. But I care about you,
whether your name is Linda or Georgi, and whatever has
shaped you into the person you are today. I care about
whatever dreams you have for your life, and now that I've*

found you, I want to help you achieve those dreams. I know that it will take time for you to get to know me, but I hope that you'll give me a chance to show you the seriousness of my commitment to you.

They were all crying now and Linda had to put down the letter to get some tissues.

After blowing her nose, Mary said, "Do they even make men like him anymore?"

Chris said, "We have to go talk to him."

"You'll go with me?" Linda asked.

"Of course we'll go with you," Mary said. "Tomorrow."

"What else does the letter say?" Chris asked.

Picking it up again, Linda said, "He gives me the phone number where he's staying downtown and his home and office numbers in Pittsburgh in case I don't go talk to him here, and he says he will defer to my wishes on what I want. He signs it *'The Father You Didn't Know You Had, Andrew'*"

"Wow, I have to tell Chuck," Chris said, getting up to go to the phone.

"This is just like a Hollywood movie," Mary said. "Who would have thought our plain old middle-class family had such a huge dark secret?"

"Our family had so many secrets, who the hell knows what the truth is?" Linda said angrily, getting up to clear away the coffee cups.

"I wish we could call Andrew now," Mary said, looking at her watch. "Oh my gosh, it's after midnight." Getting her purse, she said, "Come on, Chris, we have to go. Call me first thing in the morning, Linda, and we'll go see Andrew."

Chris hung up the phone and said, "I'm calling in sick tomorrow. I want to go with you."

Linda groaned, remembering work. She hadn't called them to explain why she didn't go back after lunch and she was going to have to talk to them in the morning and make up a story. "All right, I'll see you tomorrow," she called after her sisters as they left, then sat back down and picked up Andrew's letter.

Chapter Thirteen

It was one of those rare winter days in Cleveland that was sunny. Chris was remarking on that fact as she drove Linda and Mary down the Shoreway towards town in post-rush-hour traffic. "The lake is so blue and sparkly today," she said, glancing to her left.

Chris was acting like they were going downtown on some fun shopping excursion, Linda thought, feeling like her nerves were jumping around inside her much like the sun flecks were skipping on the waves.

Linda had tried on just about every outfit in her closet, trying to decide what she should wear to meet Andrew. She finally asked herself why the hell she was so nervous and threw on a pair of jeans and a turtleneck. Her sisters had arrived wearing wool slacks and chided her, saying that the Sheraton was a fancy hotel and they didn't know if they'd even let her in wearing jeans.

"In all the years I've lived in Cleveland, I've never even stepped foot in that hotel," Chris said.

"I would have worn a dress, but it's too darn cold," Mary said.

"This is what I'm wearing, so live with it," Linda said moodily.

She had forced Mary to call her boss and tell him she had gotten food poisoning at lunch the day before and was still very sick. She knew she was being a coward and remembered Andrew's words to be courageous, but decided she would save her strength for the important stuff. *Like now*, she thought, as they pulled into the garage of the hotel and parked.

"What did Andrew say when you called him?" she asked Mary.

"I told you," Mary said. "He was happy to hear from me and told us to come as soon as we could get here this morning."

"What am I going to say to him?" Linda asked.

"How about hello?" Chris said dryly, locking the car doors and starting towards the entrance.

"I'm serious," Linda said, now wanting to go back home. She lagged behind them in the lobby. "I don't know if this was such a good idea."

"It'll be fine," Mary said, holding the elevator door open. "Come on before this thing closes on me."

"Wow, I'm sinking down to my ankles in this carpet!" Chris exclaimed as they walked down the hall to Andrew's door.

Mary, who was reading off the numbers on the doors, stopped and said, "Here it is."

They all looked at each other, Linda nervously wiping her sweaty palms on her coat. Mary, as usual, took the bull by the horns and knocked on the door. Almost immediately it was opened by Andrew, who was grinning from ear to ear.

"Come in, come in," he stepped aside. "I'm so glad to see you." Winking at them he asked, "Did you all play hooky from work today?"

While they nodded dumbly, he said, "So did I, except, as you can see," gesturing towards the dining room table, "I'm working on a speech I have to write for the promotion of a new machine we're getting ready to market. Let me clear off the table and make a fresh pot of coffee while you hang up your coats."

Calling out to them, he asked, "Are you hungry? Would you like me to call downstairs and order some breakfast?"

"No, thank you," they answered politely.

"What machine is your speech about?" Mary asked conversationally, sitting down at the table Andrew had cleared. "Uncle Robbie talks about work a lot and told us he was working on something new."

"As a matter of fact," Andrew said, "it's the new DNA blood testing machine that Robert helped develop. He has been a big help to me, not only with this, but also in leading me to you."

"So Uncle Robbie knows too?" Chris asked. "He never said."

"He's the only one in your family who knows," Andrew said, turning his attention to Chris. "We decided to keep it discreet and give you all some time to get over the shock."

"What did Uncle Robbie tell you?" Mary asked.

Andrew got up to get the coffee that had finished brewing. Pouring it into their cups, he said, "He was just as shocked as all of you are, I can tell you that. But he did help a lot by filling in some of the gaps."

"How?" Mary persisted.

Sitting back down, Andrew said, "He told me that Pat was pregnant when she and Mike arrived at his house for their father's funeral, which was to be held the next day. He hadn't seen her in almost a year, not since she and Mike ran off to get married."

"Wow, I didn't know they had run away to get married," Chris said.

"Apparently there's a lot we don't know," Linda said, looking to Andrew to continue.

"Well, she was having some problems, some labor pains, and Mike wouldn't take her to the hospital. Robert thinks they didn't have insurance. In any case, Pat came downstairs in the middle of the night and Robert found her on the kitchen floor, bleeding. So he rushed her to the hospital and the next day when Mike found out, he was furious. There was a big fight and Mike left the house. The funeral was that day and no one went to the hospital. The next time Robert heard from them was later that night when Pat called and told them that she had a baby girl and they were already headed back home.

"So I *was* born that day," Linda said.

"No," Andrew said. "The baby girl Pat had was stillborn."

"We had another sister?" Mary said.

"But how did they get switched?" Chris asked. "Did Mom know?"

"She was drugged when Mike took her out of the hospital that night. She didn't know her baby had died," Andrew said.

"You found that out when you talked to Dad?" Linda asked.

"Yes," Andrew said. "Mike said that he and the doctor were going to tell Pat in the morning, so he snuck in and wheeled her out that night while she was still drugged."

"But when and how did he take your daughter?" Chris asked.

Looking at Linda, he said, "We had a party for your christening. Everyone we knew was there. We wanted to show you off," he smiled at her.

That smile was melting her heart, and with the thaw came the tears. Always-prepared-Mary pulled a box of tissues from her huge purse, took one and handed the box over to Linda.

"What else have you got in that bag of tricks?" Chris asked wryly.

Everyone laughed when Mary said, "I brought smelling salts too. Just in case."

"Anyway," Andrew continued, "it was a beautiful day and we had set up tents and tables on the lawn. Everyone was outside. Later, after the caterers had gone home and it was starting to get dark, Mae took you in to put you to bed. A few minutes later Mae's sister-in-law said she was going in too, and then we heard her screams. I ran in to see what was wrong, and Mae was lying on the floor unconscious and you were gone. It happened so fast…." he trailed off, watching his hands play with his coffee cup.

The only sounds in the room were the pulling of tissues out of its box and noses being blown. Outside, a church bell was chiming the hour and Linda involuntarily counted the chimes. Eleven.

Finally breaking the silence, Chris said, "But how did Dad know about the party? How did he do it?"

"*Why* did he do it?" Linda asked.

"He said that after the doctor told him about the dead baby, he went to a bar to figure out how he was going to tell

Pat," Andrew said. "He ran into an old friend of his, an ex-employee of mine, who had been at our party."

"I just can't imagine him doing anything like that!" Linda exclaimed.

"Desperation makes people do terrible things," Andrew said.

"You seem willing to excuse him!" Chris said.

Andrew looked around at the horror on their faces and felt sympathy for these girls who were trying to grapple with what Mike had done, their pain and disappointment so evident. He knew that kids saw their parents as gods, thinking they could do no wrong. He had been damned fortunate, he thought once again. He never had to experience the hurt and betrayal he saw in their eyes right now.

The only thing he could say was, "Parents are just like everyone else, they're just people. Some are weaker than others. They make mistakes."

As they mulled over the unbelievable, he got up and said, "I'm going to order us some sandwiches, I've had way too much coffee. Is there anything special you'd like?"

"Anything is fine," Mary said, answering for them all. "I've got to use the restroom."

"Help yourself," Andrew called over his shoulder as he dialed room service.

Chris walked to the window, crossing her arms in front of her angrily, as if she was trying to hold them back from punching a hole in the wall.

Linda wanted a cigarette in the worst way. She was just about to sneak downstairs when Andrew came back and asked her if she'd like a soda.

"I would," Mary said, coming out of the bathroom. "Whatever you have is fine."

Trying to grapple with the lies blurring the facts, Linda asked, "Did he really shoot himself?"

"Yes, but I think it was more to avoid the slow death of cancer than guilt over what he had done. He just wanted to get it off his chest before he died," Andrew speculated, "and put it right by you. He told me to tell you he was sorry."

After a long silence, Linda said, "I keep having this same dream over and over, that he had locked himself in the basement with a gun and was threatening to shoot himself."

"That's not a dream," Mary said. "That really happened. I overheard Mom telling someone. But when I asked her about it, she denied it."

"Did Mom give him the gun?" Chris asked. "I mean this time, in California?"

"That's what everyone thinks, but no one knows for sure," Andrew said. His heart went out to these girls who didn't know what to believe.

"But did she go visit him in California?" Linda asked.

"Yes." Andrew said. "The nursing home said she was there the week before me."

"So she knew where he was and she knew he was sick, even though she told me she didn't," Linda said feebly. "Maybe she knew all along about me, too."

"I don't think so," Andrew said. "When I told her what Mike said, she got extremely rattled and wouldn't believe me."

"She always defended him," Chris said.

"That's what Robert said too," Andrew concurred. "I think it really hit her when I told her about your birthmark." Looking intently at the three girls, he said, "I'm really sorry that she took it so hard. I've wondered how I could have said it differently, or done it differently, but…"

"We don't blame you, Andrew," Mary cut him off.

Looking at Linda and Chris nodding their heads in agreement, he smiled gratefully. "Thank you."

There was a knock on the door and Andrew said, "Oh good, our lunch is here."

When he stepped away to answer the door, Chris said, "Now I understand how Mom would rather die than admit to this screw-up."

"Chris!" Mary shouted.

"What's wrong?" Andrew asked, setting a tray of sandwiches and chips on the table.

"Oh nothing," Mary giggled. "Chris was just being her normal macabre self."

Andrew smiled at them, "Help yourselves, ladies," and went for plates and napkins.

"Now there's a word," Chris said, duly impressed. Inspecting the sandwich tray, she asked, "What does that mean, anyway?"

"It means you're shockingly horrible," Mary said, punctuating the statement by taking a big bite of chicken salad.

"I'm shocked you're so horrible," Andrew joked as he grabbed a sandwich for himself and sat down.

They all laughed, loosening the tension in the room, and Linda realized she was famished. "Thank you for lunch," she said to Andrew, taking a sandwich for herself.

Her sisters nodded their gratitude with full mouths, and Andrew said with mock formality, "It is my great honor to have you ladies dine with me today."

Linda giggled, but then got self-conscious at the way he was looking at her.

"I love hearing you laugh," he said with pleasure and pride at having wrestled a giggle out of her.

"You should hear her when she really gets going," Chris said. "She snorts!"

They all laughed at that, but Linda was getting embarrassed, feeling like a spotlight had been turned on her.

Andrew changed the course of their conversation, saying, "I'm glad to see you girls are so close. I don't know what I'd ever do without my sister, Judy."

Chris gave a short laugh. "That's the first time anyone has accused us of being close," she said.

Mary was thoughtful. "Since Mom died, we've gotten a lot closer."

It was true, Linda thought. If their mom was still alive, she doubted that her sisters would be rallying around her like they had been the last couple of days. They had all instinctively known that treating Linda any differently than their mom did would have been viewed as traitorous.

Linda could tell they were all thinking along the same lines when Mary said, "I think Mom must have had some idea that something wasn't right."

"What do you mean?" Andrew asked.

"Maybe her theory was to divide and conquer," Linda said, not wanting to get into the discussion again about the way her mother had treated her.

"Maybe," Chris said, "but I think Mary is right in believing that Mom knew something wasn't as it should be. She was always angry at you, it seemed."

"Robert said something to that effect too and I'm sorry to hear it," Andrew said. "I tend to agree, though, that she had some nagging inclination but couldn't admit it to herself."

Linda felt vaguely vindicated that she hadn't been paranoid about her mother's feelings, but another part of her was appalled that it had been so blatant that even Uncle Robbie had noticed. If it wasn't her imagination and her mother really hated her as much as Linda thought she did, then she couldn't deny the fact that her mother had killed herself because of her, not because of her father's death. She turned her head toward the window, hiding the tears she couldn't control.

"Are you all right?" Andrew asked.

The same question he had asked her at the funeral home with all the concern in his voice that had made her want to fall into his arms. She had pushed him away then but now she didn't have the strength or desire to resist. She looked down at her lap and mumbled, "I tried," she sobbed, "to make her love me."

Andrew was on his feet and at her side in less than a second. He pulled her into his arms, holding her tight and whispering in her ear, "It's all right, sweetie. It's all right. How could anyone not love you?"

"It's my fault," she cried into his shoulder. "I didn't try hard enough. She killed herself because of me. And Dad too, he left because of me."

"No, baby, no," he said, as he held her and let her cry.

In time, Linda's sobs subsided and Andrew backed up a step in order to take her face in his hands. Looking at her intently, he said, "If they didn't love you, it was because of their own weakness. Not yours. You shouldn't have to try to make anyone love you," he said.

In her embarrassment, she started to move away, but Andrew wrapped her in his arms again and said, "I've loved you since before you were born and I will love you forever." Adding solemnly, "I promise you that."

Linda gave into him and put her arms around him, hugging him back, hoping against all hope that it was true; that she really was the daughter he loved and searched for; that this wonderful, sensitive, loving man was really her father.

Chris blew her nose and said, "Oh, I wish I had brought my camera!"

"Lucky for me," Linda said, excusing herself to go to the restroom.

Splashing water on her face, she tried to let the meaning of his words sink in. It was too much to comprehend, but she was becoming resolved to finding the truth. If she really was Andrew's daughter, she wanted to know.

They were cleaning up the remains of lunch when she returned. Andrew straightened up from putting some trash in a bag and searched her face for clues on how she was faring. What he saw in her delicate features was determination, and he thought for a minute that she was going to pick up her purse and walk out the door.

Instead, she sat back down at the table, too immersed in her own thoughts to register that she should help them and asked, "Andrew, what about my birth certificate?"

Relieved she wasn't thinking of running, Andrew came and sat down beside her. "The birth certificate you have has never been registered. Apparently, no one ever checked."

"Dad must have gotten someone to fake it," Chris said.

"I have your birth certificate," Andrew said. "You were born Georgia Marie Lexington on August 4, 1961."

"Why that's almost a month earlier!" Mary exclaimed. "Wouldn't someone be able to tell a month old baby from a newborn?"

"You were very tiny," Andrew explained.

Chris finished cleaning up and came back to the table. Pouring more soda, she said, "Don't think you're going to have two birthdays from now on."

Laughing, but not wanting to be distracted, Linda said to Andrew, "You told Mary that you had a death certificate?"

"I have it right here," Andrew said, as he dug it out of his briefcase. Handing it to her, he said, "Mike told the doctor what they planned on naming their baby."

Linda looked at her name and date of death imprinted on the certificate and gave a shudder.

"Freaky," Mary said, peering over her shoulder.

"I know it's hard to comprehend," Andrew said compassionately, as Linda continued to stare at the paper. "But Linda died that day."

"Let me see," Chris said, reaching out for it."

Handing it over the table to her, Linda said softly, "The person I thought I was died?"

"It's just a name," Chris said, putting the paper down on the table.

"It's more than the name...." Linda was trying to find the words to explain.

"It was your identity," Andrew finished for her.

"Yes," she whispered.

After some thought, Andrew said, "Well, you still have something tangible and real that tells you who you are."

"What's that?" she asked.

"The birthmark you've had since the day you were born. Do you still have it, or did you have it removed?"

"She still has it!" Mary shouted. "Show him!"

Blushing, while everyone else laughed, she shook her head.

Amused, Andrew said, "I've seen it. It proves your identity, Georgi."

"I'm sure there are other people with a birthmark in the same place," she said practically.

"As I recall," Andrew said smiling, "yours is unique. It looks like a handprint."

Giggling, she nodded. This was surreal.

"To think you always hated that mark, and it turns out to be the one thing that proves who you really are," Mary said.

"There is one other way," Andrew said.

"What?" she and Chris asked in tandem.

"DNA testing," Andrew said. "It's the new product I was telling you about. The one I'm giving a speech on next week."

Mary said, "That's supposed to tell you if people are related, right?

Nodding, Andrew said, "People related by blood have similar chromosome patterns. This machine matches them up."

"So if Linda is your daughter, it would show that," Mary finished.

"Yes." Andrew smiled at Linda. "Care to donate a little blood to science?"

"How?" Linda asked nervously.

"All we need is a little pin prick on your finger," Andrew said.

"Oh, go ahead," Chris nudged.

Andrew looked at Linda. When she nodded, he got up to rummage through his briefcase again.

"Talk about *my* bag of tricks," Chris said, when Andrew brought back a glass vial and laid it on the table.

"Do you have a safety pin and some matches in that bag?" he asked Chris.

Digging around, Chris produced a safety pin and said, "I have a pin but no matches."

"I have matches," Linda said, pulling them out of her purse and handing them to Andrew.

He sterilized the pin and held out his hand for hers. "This will only hurt for a second," he said.

She gave him her hand and looked away, but it was over before she knew it and hadn't hurt much at all.

"Okay now, all you have to do is squeeze a couple drops into this vial," he said as he held it out in front of her.

Carefully, she did what he asked and then took a tissue to dab at her finger. "That was easy," she said triumphantly.

"When will we know?" Chris asked.

Andrew put some tape on the vial and was writing her name on it. Linda watched him write "Georgia Lexington." He held it up and showed it to her, smiling. She had to smile back at his boyish enthusiasm.

"It will only take a few days," he said. "I've got an 'in' at the lab," he winked.

"Can we test ours too?" Mary asked. "That way we'll have a comparison between the Bigelow and Lexington blood."

"I'm not doing that," Chris stated emphatically. "What if we find out that another one of us isn't a Bigelow?"

Mary looked at her in alarm. Then she laughed and said, "Of course we're Bigelows, silly. There are only so many secrets a family can keep! Besides, don't you want to know?"

Looking at Mary, he said, "I'd be happy to have yours tested too so you won't have any lingering doubts about your identity."

When she eagerly nodded her consent, he went back to his briefcase to retrieve another vial.

Chris's curiosity got the better of her. "Do you have another one of those things in there?" she asked Andrew. When Linda and Mary both arched a look at her, she shrugged and said, "I guess it would be good to know."

Linda was thinking that if she really was Georgi, it would explain so much. Like why she had never seen any pictures of the day she was born. Their mother had tons of pictures of Mary and Chris in the hospital right after their birth. When she asked her about it, her mother said that things were just too hectic that day. Now, hearing Andrew's explanation, she understood.

Andrew was labeling both her sisters' samples when she asked him, "Do you have any pictures of the day Georgi..er..I was born?"

Grinning, he said, "Sure do. I have pictures of you in the hospital nursery. I have pictures of your mom holding you for the first time. I have tons of pictures. I also have the required naked picture," he laughed. "I even have a picture of your birthmark. If you'll come to our house this weekend, I'll show them all to you."

"Really?" she asked.

"We should have the results of these tests by then," he said. "What do you say?"

"She doesn't have a car," Chris explained. "But I could drive her. Do you mind if Chuck and I came too?"

"By all means, please do," he answered. "Like I told Robert, we're family now."

They all grinned at him, except Mary, who was pouting.

"Do you and your husband want to come too, Mary? We've got plenty of room."

"I have to go to that stupid wedding," she said to the girls. To Andrew she explained, "Someone Bill works with and we already told them we'd be there."

"There's a weekend at the end of every week," Andrew said, smiling at her, "and you're welcome to come for every one of them if you'd like."

"You are just the kindest person I've ever met," Mary said, getting up to give him a hug.

Holding on to her and giving her a tight squeeze, he said, "Bigelow or Lexington, you girls are sisters and always will be."

Mary backed away from him, wiping her eyes, she said, "That's what we were saying last night!"

"It's true," Andrew said. Looking at Linda, he added, "and whether you want to be called Linda or Georgi, you're still my daughter."

"We should call you Georgi," Mary said. "That's what your birth certificate says."

"We could try it on for size," Chris said. Looking at her watch, she added, "but I need to get going. I promised Chuck I'd make him lasagna tonight and I've got to go to the grocery store."

"They're newlyweds," Mary said to Andrew by way of explanation.

Chuckling, he pulled Mary into another hug and said, "Thank you for coming."

"No problem," Mary said, following Chris to the coat closet. "And I'm going to take you up on your offer to visit."

"Please do," Andrew said, helping Chris on with her coat and hugging her too. "I'll see you this weekend. I'll call you with the directions."

"Here, Georgi let me help you," he said, taking the side of her coat that didn't have an arm in it yet.

She giggled and he pulled her into a hug. "Thank you for hearing me out," he said.

She nodded into his shoulder and he said, "We've got so many years to catch up on. I can't wait for you to come to our house this weekend. I want to learn all about you."

Nodding again, she stepped back and smiled up at him. "Thank you, Andrew."

Their eyes connected and locked in a moment of mutual recognition that felt primal. Both of their eyes filled with tears as Andrew said softly, "You're welcome, Georgi."

Chapter Fourteen

Linda got to work the next day and barely had time to hang up her coat when her boss called her into his office. *Here it comes*, she thought, taking her time getting there.

"What's wrong?" she asked him, knowing full well what his answer would be.

"Your unexcused absences, that's what's wrong," Doug Lamont said, glaring at her. "You left for lunch Monday and never came back. Never even called."

"But I was really sick," she lied.

"Yeah," Doug said, "you've been really sick too many times this year already and it's only January. I'm going to have to write you up again Linda. Do you know what that means?"

"I'm fired?" she asked.

"You've been written up twice now. One more and you're out," he glowered.

"I'm sorry, it won't happen again," she said.

"It better not," Doug said. "You know everyone else has to do your work for you when you're gone and we've all got too much to do as it is."

"I know. I'm sorry," she said again, getting up to escape his office.

"One more thing," he stopped her when her hand was on the doorknob.

"Yes?" she turned to face him again.

"Are the rumors about you and Tom true?" he asked.

"I...uh...don't think that's relevant," she stammered.

"It's relevant," he said raising his voice, "when there's a no fraternization policy and it causes discord in the office."

"Well, it's over," she said humiliated, and then got out before he could stop her again.

Jake's roses still sat on her desk. She had forgotten they would be there to greet her this morning. She flopped into her chair and stared at them, wanting to cry. She had tried calling him several times yesterday afternoon but he never returned her calls. She thought for sure he would call her last night when he got home from work, but he hadn't. The last time she had talked to him was outside her apartment that night he went away angry. She had probably blown it with the one guy who cared enough about her to send her flowers.

Yesterday had been life changing. And yet, here she was today in her same old dreary life. She had been so excited to tell Jake; sure that once he knew all the facts, he wouldn't feel threatened by Andrew anymore.

Though, waiting by the phone last night, her excitement was being replaced by fear incrementally in the tick of the clock. She may never hear from him again. Never be able to explain and make it right. Thinking of Doug's warnings, she sighed and started in on the pile of work on her desk.

An hour and a half later, her phone rang and Jake said, "You're there. I thought you had quit and left town."

"Oh Jake," she exclaimed. "I'm so happy you called. I tried calling you yesterday."

"Really?" he said nonchalantly. "I never got a message."

She thought a minute and said, "But I left two at your store. They said you were with a customer."

"So why didn't you go to work yesterday?" he asked.

"I have so much to tell you, Jake. I'll explain it all. Can you come over for dinner tonight? I'll cook."

"That will be a first," he said wryly. "Okay then, I'll see you tonight."

~ ~ ~ ~

Linda got off the bus at the grocery store, two stops before her apartment. She was browning the meat to add to her spaghetti sauce when Jake knocked. Opening the door, she threw herself into his arms.

Laughing, he said, "Now there's a welcome for you. I'm glad to see you're in a better mood than you were the other day."

"I've missed you so much," she said, giving him a kiss. "Do you like spaghetti?"

"Smells good," Jake said, taking his coat off and laying it over the back of a chair. "So why didn't you go to work yesterday?"

She put the water on the stove to boil, wondering again how she was going to explain this impossible story. Nothing to do but dive right in, she thought. "I know you're not going to believe this," she began, "because I didn't at first either, but there is a lot of evidence to suggest that I'm Andrew's daughter." Looking at his face that seemed to say "I knew it," she continued. "When Chris and Mary were here Monday night, we read a letter that Andrew had given me and we decided that we should go talk to him. I mean, what could it hurt to find out the facts, right?" She could see Jake's irritation level rising like high tide, so she hurried on. Talking faster, she said, "So we went to see him and he told us what my dad <u>told</u> him before he died; that he had stolen me out of Andrew's house and replaced me for the stillborn baby my mother had delivered. He had this dead baby's death certificate, Jake, and it had my name on it!"

"Anybody can fake a death certificate, Linda," he snapped, coming over to lift the heavy pot to help her drain the pasta. "And anyone can say anything they want about what your dad said. He's dead. He can't dispute it."

Getting plates out of the cupboard, she said, "But that's not all. He described my birthmark perfectly, Jake."

"Sure he hasn't seen it before?" Jake asked, swatting her butt with the dishtowel a little too hard to be playful.

"Jake! That hurt!"

After they had settled into eating their dinner, she asked, "So what did you do last night?"

"Nothing much," he said. "Just went out for a couple drinks."

"Where? With whom?" she asked.

"Now who's the jealous one?" he asked, winking at her.

"I'm not jealous," she said, feeling more hurt that he hadn't called her than jealous.

"Not even a little?" he asked, grinning, almost as if that had been his goal.

Not wanting to sour his playful mood with her bruised feelings, she acquiesced and said, "Well, maybe a little."

After dinner, Jake stood and took both of her hands in his, willing her to stand. "Come here," he said, "we can clean this mess up later." He piloted her into the bedroom and pulled her down on top of him on the bed.

"How can you think about sex when our stomachs are so full?" she laughed.

"I'll show you how," he said, pulling her shirt off.

Lying contentedly in his arms later, she felt her world was finally right again. Jake loved her.

"What are you thinking about?" he asked, propping himself up on one elbow and running a lazy finger along her hairline.

Smiling up at him, she said, "That I missed you."

"Ummmm," he murmured, kissing her. "That's my girl."

"Jake?"

"Umm?" he asked, kissing her again.

"Would you go with me to Andrew's house this weekend?"

Pulling back and looking at her, he asked, "Why?"

"Well, because he invited us and also because I took a blood test and the results will be in by then."

Jake was sitting up now, feeling for the pants he had thrown on the floor. "Can't he just call you with the results?"

Linda was sitting up too, clutching the sheet around her. "But he wants to show me some pictures too," she said, now afraid he was going to leave.

Standing and pulling his pants up, exasperated, he said, "You're just not going to let this drop, are you Linda? Not waiting for an answer, he continued. "What are you thinking? That you'll be able to re-live your childhood with your new daddy?"

Stunned at the bite in his voice, she stammered, "I...I just want to know who I am."

Sitting down on the edge of the bed and speaking in a patient voice that belied his words, he said, "You're an adult, Linda. That's who you are. An adult who has a life of her own now. I was hoping that it would be a life with me, not your daddy." He stood up again to put his shirt on.

Rising, she wrapped her arms around his waist, effectively stopping him from buttoning his shirt. He didn't return her embrace, letting his arms hang limply at his sides. Pleading with him not to be angry, she said, "I do want a life with you, Jake."

Turning and removing her arms, he said, "That's my girl." He kissed the top of her head and resumed the buttoning of his shirt. Linda was wrapping her bathrobe around herself when a new thought lit up his face and he said, "Why don't we go away somewhere this weekend? Just you and me."

She was disappointed that he didn't want to go to Andrew's house but what he said was true; she was an adult now, whoever her father was.

When she didn't answer him right away, Jake turned and walked into the kitchen to start cleaning up the dinner dishes. Linda followed him and said, "I'll clean this up later, Jake. Where did you want to go?"

"We could go to Niagara Falls," he said. "It's beautiful there in the winter." When she looked at him doubtfully, he added, "It would be so romantic, Linda. We could get one of those hotel rooms with a heart-shaped tub."

"That's where people go on their honeymoon," she giggled.

Warming to his plan, Jake said, "We can practice for our honeymoon, but on our real honeymoon I'm going to take you somewhere much more exotic."

Caught off guard, Linda sat down on one of the kitchen chairs. Serious now, she said, "What are you saying Jake? Do you think we'll get married someday?"

Taking her hand and sitting down beside her, Jake said, "Of course we're going to get married Linda. What do you think this is all about?"

"Oh, I've thought about it," she confessed. "Everybody thinks 'what if we got married' while they're dating. But it's so soon, we don't know each other that well." She was protesting, yet thinking, *he wants to marry me!*

"I know I love you and that's all I need to know," Jake said. "Just think, I wouldn't have to leave and go home and we could be together all the time. I don't want to be alone anymore, Linda, and I know you don't either," he said earnestly.

"No, I don't want to be alone," she agreed. "But....."

"But what, Linda?" he asked, dropping her hand and standing up.

Looking up at him with pleading eyes, she said, "It's just so much to think about right now."

Feeling rebuked, he yanked his coat off the back of the chair and put it on. "Well then, you best think about it, Linda, because I don't see any point in continuing something that isn't going anywhere."

Panicked, she rose and said, "Please don't be mad, Jake. I just need some time to think is all."

Conceding, Jake said, "All right, you think about it." He gave her a light kiss on the lips before turning for the door. "But don't keep me waiting too long," he said as he left.

~ ~ ~ ~

Chris called Linda at work the next day to tell her that Andrew had given her directions to his house.

"Do we have to go this weekend?" Linda asked forlornly.

"Why?" Chris demanded. "You're not chickening out, are you?"

"No, I want to go," she said, "but just not this weekend. Jake wants to take me to Niagara Falls this weekend."

"We promised Andrew," Chris said, "and he's so excited. You should have heard him on the phone last night. You and Jake can go to Niagara Falls anytime."

Frustrated, Linda shouted, "Why is everyone trying to force me to make a decision about this?"

"Nobody is forcing you to do anything, Linda," Chris said, sounding a lot like their mother. Softening her tone, she asked, "Why? Is Jake forcing you to change your plans for the weekend?"

After a thoughtful moment, Linda said, "Not exactly. Well, kind of, but he's right. How is knowing who my biological father is going to change my life? I'm still me and this is still my life no matter what my birth certificate says."

"I don't get it," Chris said. "Does he expect you to just ignore this? What's his problem?"

"I think he wants to get married and make a life with me and all this other stuff just gets in the way, like I've got too much baggage or something," Linda said.

"Married?" Chris exclaimed. "You just met him!"

Linda hurried to explain, "I know, but he's thinking about down the road, like where we're headed."

"Sounds to me like he's leading you down that road and ignoring what you want," Chris said.

"But I want to be with him," Linda whined. "I love him, and he loves me."

"Does he love you enough to let you find out who you are?" Chris asked.

"Oh stop it!" Linda said. "I don't know. I don't want to lose him, Chris," she said miserably. "I think that if I go to Andrew's this weekend, it will be the end of us."

"I can't believe he's giving you an ultimatum like that." Chris said. "That would do it for me. I'd tell him to hit the road."

"Easy for you to say," Linda moaned. "You're not in love with him."

"You can say that again!" Chris said. "Right now, I don't even like him. With the little tantrum he threw the other night and now the way he's trying to manipulate you, he reminds me of Jim."

"He's nothing like Jim!" Linda shouted, thinking of how her ex-husband had walked all over her. "Jake loves me, he wouldn't hurt me."

"He can say whatever he wants to say, but it's his actions I'm concerned about," Chris said. "You need to grow a backbone and stand up to him. He's forcing you to make a choice, so that's what you'll have to do."

Muttering that she would think about it, Linda hung up the phone and stared at the flowers Jake had sent her. Several of them were hanging their little heads in mourning.

Chapter Fifteen

Chuck was loading Linda's overnight bag into the trunk of his car Saturday morning, when Linda came outside and saw a car that looked like Jake's. It was backed into a parking space so that the front faced her. She stopped so abruptly that Chris, who was behind her, ran into her back.

"What's wrong?" Chris asked, watching Linda stare across the parking lot.

The early morning light was reflecting off the car's front window, not allowing Linda to see into it – although she was able to discern the outline of a person sitting in the driver's seat. "I think that's Jake," she said. Then changing her mind she said, "But it can't be him because he's not getting out."

Chris shuttered and said, "Come on, let's get in the car and go. If that's Jake, it's really creepy that he's just sitting there watching us."

Whoever it was, Linda could feel him staring at her. She raised her hand in a feeble wave and waited for some type of response. Nothing. Getting into the backseat of Chuck's car, she said, "Yeah, let's get out of here."

When Chuck backed the car out of his parking space, Linda didn't raise her eyes, even though she might have a better angle from which to see. If it was him, she didn't want to know. Nor did she want to see the betrayal on his face.

When they pulled into the street, Chris looked back and asked, "Was it him?"

"Who?" Chuck asked, feeling like he had missed something.

"That guy Linda's been dating," Chris said by way of explanation to Chuck, but looking at Linda, waiting for an answer.

Linda gave an I-don't-know-and-I-don't-care shrug, as Chuck persisted in trying to find out what he had missed.

"Where?" he asked.

"Back there in the parking lot. He was just sitting in his car staring at us. I'm pretty sure it was him."

"But why would he just sit there?" Chuck looked at Linda in the rearview mirror, eyebrows raised.

"It's a long story," Linda said, not knowing where to begin filling him in on the events of the past week.

He was a curious guy and always wanted details. Luckily, Chris had already filled him in on most of the story, at least the part she knew. He switched tactics and guessed, "You told him you decided to go to Andrew's house this weekend and he got mad."

"Not exactly," Linda said, even though that was basically what she had told Chris. "I didn't know what to do. But then

Jill called and said that she saw Jake at the bar the other night with another girl."

"When was that?" Chris asked, spinning around.

"The day we talked to Andrew at the hotel. He was upset with me from the night before, when you and Mary were there."

"So he gets mad at you and goes out with another girl?" Chris asked. "What a creep."

"But Jake told me he wasn't with another girl that night," Linda said. "He said that Jill is mistaken."

"Jake is kind of a hard guy to mistake," Chris said. "He's so tall, he stands out in a crowd."

"That's what Jill said." Chris was confirming what Linda was thinking; that Jill described Jake perfectly, even though she had only seen him one time. Even worse, she said that Jake had been so totally absorbed in the girl he was with, he hadn't noticed Jill staring at him. Just like the night she had met Jake and he had been so totally absorbed in her. It hurt her too much to think about it. She wanted to believe Jake; wanted to believe Jill was mistaken, and she told Chris so.

"It's easier for me to believe that Jake, who may have something to hide, would deny it, than that Jill is mistaken," Chris said.

"I never met the guy," Chuck said, "but he seems pretty sneaky if he's hanging out in your parking lot stalking you."

"IF it was him," Linda said, unable to believe what they were thinking about Jake. "He's not what you're making him out to be. I think he's just threatened by this whole Andrew thing, afraid that I'll change or something. He was so sweet the other night. He said that if this is what I had to do, then I should do it."

"Was that before or after you confronted him about being with another girl?" Chris asked sarcastically.

Chuck glanced through the rearview mirror at Linda, sitting with her arms crossed and looking out the window, pretending she hadn't heard the question. But her posture gave away the answer.

Three and a half hours later, Chris was reading the directions to Andrew's house as Chuck drove the unfamiliar streets. "There it is," she said excitedly, "Lexington Avenue. Can you believe he has a whole street named after him?"

"Maybe that's because their house is the only one on this street," Chuck said, looking around the tree-lined street, which basically served as a glorified driveway to the house looming ahead. Whistling through his teeth, he said, "Holy shit, would you look at that?"

He didn't need to ask. Linda and Chris were gawking at the large, stately home as Chuck slowed the car to a crawl so they could absorb it fully. The main structure had three stories rising to the sky and off each side were two story appendages that were angled in such a way as to hug the circular driveway; a driveway so large that it looked more like a cul-de-sac at the end of the street.

A light snow had fallen that morning, sprinkling the trees and shrubs. "It looks like a scene on a postcard or painting," Chris said in awe.

Linda couldn't speak around the lump in her throat. In spite of its size and classic grandeur, the house looked so homey and welcoming that it was tugging at her heartstrings.

As if in response to her heart's call, the front door burst open and Hank and Ali ran out to greet them as they pulled in the drive. "We've been waiting for you!" they screamed, hopping up and down in their excitement for Linda to get out of the car.

"You don't have any coats!" she laughed. "Let's get you inside." Looking up, she saw Andrew coming towards them wearing a smile that could warm them all. He grabbed her up into a bear hug so tight, it caused the lump in her throat to gush out through her eyes. He didn't seem to be able to speak either, but there was no need. The reunion was all the more poignant for its lack of words.

Judy, John and Mae were on Andrew's heels, giving out their own welcoming hugs and greetings. Andrew gave Linda up to the masses and went to shake Chuck's hand and help him with the luggage.

Even the usually stoic Chris was flushing from the reception they were receiving and said, "You'd think we just came home from the war or something!"

"Truer words have never been spoken," John laughed, reaching for a bag from the trunk.

"Oh, don't pay any attention to us," Mae said, wiping a tear from her eye, "Y'all come inside now, where it's warm."

"I agree," Judy said, linking her arm through Linda's. Ali grabbed Linda's other hand and pulled her toward the house. "We made a surprise for you," she chortled.

"Come and see!" shouted Hank, bounding up the stairs ahead of them.

They ascended into the house en masse until Linda stopped dead in her tracks. A large home-made banner which said, "Welcome Home Georgi!" was hung across the upstairs railing that ran the length of the hall.

"Do you like it?" Ali asked anxiously.

Linda stared at the sign they had gone to so much trouble to make and then, looking down at her expectant face, said, "I love it!" Kneeling to give both children a hug of gratitude, she murmured, "Thank you!"

"They've been working on that sign for days," Andrew said proudly, coming in behind them and dropping luggage on the floor.

"You did a beautiful job," Chris said to the children. Turning to Andrew, she asked, "Does this mean you got the results of the blood test?"

He winked and said, "I did."

"And it proves that Linda really *is* Georgi?" Chris asked, as excited now as the children.

"It does," Andrew said, looking to Linda for her reaction.

"Yahoo!" Chris shouted, jumping up and down and grabbing Linda in a very uncharacteristic hug. "You're a Lexington!" she announced.

Linda laughed nervously, blushing from having every eye in the room on her. "Well, I'm not sure what being a Lexington is supposed to feel like," she stammered.

Mae snorted and said, "If you're anything like the rest of this family, you feel hungry. I've got some lunch in the kitchen that's been waiting on you."

They laughed and followed her in, but Linda was rooted to her spot on the floor, trying to make a connection with the name "Georgi" on the sign overhead.

"Come on, let's go eat," Andrew said, putting an arm around her shoulders. "It will take some time, but you'll get used to it."

Judy was bringing in a dining room chair to add to the already crowded kitchen table. She stopped to watch as Andrew and Linda walked in side by side. "It sure didn't take a blood test for me to know you two are related," she said smiling.

Andrew deposited Linda into her chair and helped Mae by lifting the pot of stew she had been simmering all morning. "We should probably save the champagne for tonight when everyone gets here," he said, setting the pot on the table.

"Who's coming tonight?" Chris asked.

"Grandma and Grandpa!" Ali yelled.

"And Uncle Ted and Aunt Denise," Hank added.

"And Robert and Laura," Judy finished.

"Uncle Robbie and Aunt Laura are coming too?" Chris asked.

"They sure are," Andrew said, spooning stew into everyone's bowls. "Mae's been cooking for days."

"And there's another surprise!" Ali yelled.

"Hush now child," Mae said, setting two steaming loaves of bread on the table. "You've surprised her to death already."

"But…." began Ali.

She was suppressed by her father putting his finger to his lips in a silencing gesture.

"Oh please," Linda laughed. "No more surprises!"

"There's plenty of time for that," Andrew said. "Dig in and after lunch, we'll show you around and get you settled in your rooms."

There was a mad flurry of salad and bread and stew being passed around the table and moans of delight as they tasted one of Mae's signature dishes.

"Can I get your recipe for this so I can make it at home?" Chris asked, after Chuck proclaimed it to be the best stew he had ever eaten in his life.

"There's no recipe," Mae said. "But later on I'll show you how to make it just like my mama showed me."

"I would owe you my life if you could teach Chris how to cook," Chuck said, but then yelped from the kick he received under the table from his wife.

Muting out the laughter and simultaneous conversations, Linda took in the room around her. It was obviously a room the family spent a lot of their time in, judging by the evidence of their bustling life everywhere she looked. There were schoolbooks and papers on the desk in the corner, along with what looked like a chore list tacked to the wall. There was school artwork magnetized to the refrigerator and a grocery list held hostage by a pink flamingo. A tiny little TV set was angled into the corner of one of the kitchen counters. The overall appearance was one of lived-in comfort portraying a happy, vibrant family.

One half of a wall was dominated by French doors leading out onto a deck that was white from a dusting of new snow. The frigid winter deck was in such sharp contrast to the warm and happy kitchen, that Linda involuntarily shuddered and brought her eyes back to the love and laughter presiding around this table, realizing with a start that someone had asked her a question. "I'm sorry, what?"

Hank repeated, "Are you going to stay here and live with us now, Georgi?"

Laughing nervously she said, "As wonderful as that sounds, honey, I've got a job and an apartment and a boyfriend back in Cleveland."

Judy came to her rescue and said to Hank, "Georgi will come and stay with us whenever she can." Then looking at Linda she added, "And if the time comes that you want to live here, we'd be ecstatic."

"Wow, thank you," she said, totally overwhelmed by the sentiment attached to the offer.

"Judy lived and worked in Cleveland for years before she finally moved back home," Andrew said.

Judy nodded in confirmation. "Yes, circumstances brought me back," she smiled at John.

"Now I'm a circumstance?" he teased.

Mae got up and started clearing the empty plates. "She just came to her senses, is all."

Chris and Linda jumped up to help Mae, but Judy rose with them and said, "You girls sit down and enjoy your guest status today. After today though," she warned with a wink, "no one is going to stop you when you want to help out."

Mae was bringing out the dessert plates when the phone rang and Andrew, being the closest to it, answered. After his 'hello' and a 'yes,' he was silent, listening and growing a frown.

A man on the other end of the line had asked if he was speaking to Andrew Lexington. After Andrew had responded in the affirmative, he said, "You're a fraud and a pervert." He then proceeded to call him several other disgusting names before finishing with, "and you're going to get what you deserve."

"Who was that?" Judy asked when he sat back down.

"Oh, just one of those telephone surveys," Andrew lied.

Mae set a dessert plate in front of Chris, and she groaned. "I'm so full. I don't think I have room for dessert, Mae."

When Mae raised an eyebrow at her as if she'd never heard of such a thing, Chuck piped up and said, "I'll eat hers. I love cake!"

"Speaking of love," Judy said to Linda, "when are we going to meet your boyfriend? I was hoping he would come with you this weekend."

"He couldn't come," Linda said.

"And he very nearly didn't let Linda come either," Chris blurted. Ignoring Linda's stare, she explained to Judy that she thought Jake was manipulative. "He even sat in her parking lot and watched us leave this morning, just to make her feel guilty about coming."

"*Do* you feel guilty?" Judy asked.

"A little," she admitted, looking again at the frozen world outside. Everything took on a different perspective in this warm kitchen, though, and she said sincerely to everyone at the table, "But I'm so glad that I did."

"Do you think he's stalking you?" Andrew asked, still ruminating on the recent phone call.

But Mae set a double layered chocolate cake in front of Linda, and a surprised "Ahhh" escaped her lips as she read the writing on top – *Welcome Home*. A single candle was burning in the middle.

"Make a wish!" Ali shouted in delight.

"My Mae," Andrew said, using his pet name for her, "you really outdid yourself with this cake. It's almost too pretty to eat!"

"It's a mighty special occasion," Mae said, pleased. "The way I see it, we've waited twenty-three years for this cake. But you best make a wish now and blow out that candle so we can eat it before it goes stale."

Linda blew, wishing with all her might that she could stay here and feel this loved forever.

~ ~ ~ ~

John and Hank volunteered to clean up the kitchen while everyone got settled in their rooms. Judy told the newlyweds, Chris and Chuck, that they could stay in the 'honeymoon' guest cottage. Mae went to get some fresh linens for Ted and Denise's room, since they were driving up from Atlanta and would be staying the night.

"I want to show Georgi her bedroom," Ali said, taking Linda's hand. "It's right next to mine!"

"All right," Andrew said. "I'll be the pack mule and take your bags upstairs."

"I only have one," Linda laughed, being pulled by Ali into the hall, "I can take it."

"I want to show you around anyway," he said, picking up the single bag left in the hall.

Upstairs, Ali ran into a bedroom, declaring, "This is my room, and see," she ran through a bathroom and came out of the room next door, "yours is right here. We share the bathroom!"

"You have a very pretty room," Linda said, admiring the little girl frills and baby dolls.

"Yours is nice too," Ali said, "but Mommy says we're going to let you pick out your own decorations."

"Judy's been working on this room all week," Andrew said from behind them. "It used to be hers before she and John took over the master bedroom."

"You mean I have my *own* room?" she asked, looking around the pretty room which featured white antique furniture sitting on rose colored carpeting. Matching night stands bordered a queen-sized bed and a long dresser shared a wall with a dressing table. An inviting over-stuffed chair sat in front of a set of double windows which looked out over the back yard.

Andrew set her bag down on a short cedar chest stationed at the end of the bed and said, "This is your house too, Georgi. It's only right that you have your own room."

"Is this the room I had when I was a baby?" she asked timidly.

"No," Andrew said. "I've taken that room for myself. Call me superstitious, but I don't want any of the children sleeping in there. Look, I kept Bears safe for you." He handed her a teddy bear that had been sitting mutely on the dressing table. "This was your favorite."

"And Mommy made the quilt out of your old baby blanket," Ali said proudly, running her hands over a pink and green patchwork quilt covering the bed.

"It's beautiful," she said, mimicking Ali's motions and feeling the rich textures.

"Your mother made the original quilt, that square in the middle, while she was pregnant with you," Andrew explained. "Judy put the hem around the outside to fit the bed."

Linda was overcome with emotion by the kindness everyone had shown. She stood dumbly by the bed, her eyes filling with tears.

Already impatient and ready to skip onto the next subject, Ali said, "Look, there's a picture of you and your mommy on the dresser."

Andrew picked up one of the two pictures that were being displayed on the dresser and handed it to her. "This is you and your mother on your christening day."

"Wasn't that the day…." she trailed off as she admired the picture. "She looks like an angel," she whispered. Her stare fixed on the beautiful woman, holding a baby wearing a little white dress. The woman was radiant; the sun putting halos in her blond hair and a healthy glow on her skin. She stood barefoot in the grass wearing the confidence of love.

"That's the last time I saw her smile like that," Andrew said wistfully.

"What happened to her?" Linda asked.

Andrew thought for a moment while Linda stared at the picture of the mother she had never known. Finally, he said, "She was a rare and amazing woman with a heart as big as the world." He stopped, feeling again the pain of her loss.

"She died of a broken heart," Ali finished, reciting what she'd been told.

Andrew continued, "Unfortunately, her heart didn't equip her for dealing with the atrocities of life. She couldn't bear to think what might have happened to you and it ate her up inside."

"She got cancer," Ali explained.

"Another death," Linda murmured.

"Mommy!" Ali exclaimed to Judy, who had appeared in the doorway, "Georgi likes her room."

Linda smiled at Judy. "I do love it. Thank you. The quilt is amazing."

"You're welcome," Judy said. "More than anything, I...," glancing at Andrew she corrected herself, "we all want you to feel at home here."

At a loss for words, Linda could only say, "How could I not? You're all so kind."

Speaking to Ali, Judy said, "Mae wants you to help her get ready for the party tonight."

"What about the other surprise?" Ali asked.

"There's lots of time for surprises," Andrew winked. Giving Linda a kiss on the cheek, he said, "Come on Ali, we'll let your mom get Georgi settled in while we go help with the party." At the door, he turned and motioned to the picture in Linda's hands and said, "I can feel your mother giving us one of her radiant smiles today."

"You've made him a very happy man," Judy said, sitting down on the edge of the bed and patting beside her for Linda to sit.

Linda obeyed the silent command and sat down beside Judy. *This woman had a way of making her feel so comfortable*, she thought, and then blurted out the nagging thought that had been wanting to burst out of her since her arrival. "But I haven't done anything. I'm just me, Linda Bigelow. I feel like a fake; an imposter posing as Andrew's long-lost daughter."

Judy put her arms around her and let her cry on her shoulder. Consoling her, she said, "I can't imagine any other way that you could feel right now." Then a smile came into her voice, "Unless you really *are* an imposter."

Linda pulled away to peer at Judy through her tears, seeing a twinkle in her eyes. She couldn't believe Judy wasn't angry with her for her outburst, after all she had done to make her feel welcomed. Judy's acceptance urged her on, "But I don't deserve any of this," she said, motioning around the room.

Gently pushing a lock of hair out of Linda's eyes, Judy said, "Do you think any of us deserves it? I have a wonderful life with a husband who loves me and two beautiful children. We live in this lovely home that my grandfather, your great-grandfather, built. Do I deserve all this?"

"Well, yes," Linda said hesitantly. "You belong here."

Judy smiled at her and said, "And so do you." She looked at the teddy bear and the picture Linda was still clutching and said, "I know you don't remember being that little girl your mother is holding or loving Bears or sleeping under this quilt, but you were born into this family." Judy hesitated, deep in thought. "When you were taken, we were devastated. But I've come to realize that you lost more than we did. You lost your identity."

Linda gazed at the picture of the two strangers staring back at her, trying to feel some connection to the innocent child in the little white dress or any remembrance of the beautiful woman with the dazzling smile. "I thought I knew who I was," she said softly.

"Were you happy?" Judy asked tenderly.

"Happy?" Linda repeated, confused, and wondering if she had ever been asked that question before. "I don't know," she stammered, "sometimes."

"Do you want to know how I see you?" Judy asked.

Linda nodded, grateful that she didn't have to answer any more hard questions.

"I see you as a sweet, sensitive woman whom I'm proud to call my niece," Judy said.

Linda blushed and looked down at her lap.

"And," Judy continued, "one who has a hard time accepting a compliment."

They both laughed as Judy continued. "I think you have a lot of guilt and anger bottled up inside you, and I know that you have a lot of things to work through, but we've got time and patience. All we want is for you to be happy."

"I know," Linda said sheepishly, "I didn't mean to sound ungrateful."

"You didn't," Judy said. "You sound confused, but that's to be expected. I'm glad that you can just be you and say what you feel."

"You guys are the greatest," Linda said sincerely. "You've all gone to so much trouble for me."

"It may seem like trouble to you," Judy said, "but to us, it's pure joy in having you back. I know it may be a bit overwhelming, but I hope you'll indulge us a little," she smiled.

Judy got up and took the other picture off the dresser, handing it to Linda. "This is a family photo taken on your christening day."

Looking at the group shot, Linda said, "You all look so young. Why is Andrew scowling like that?"

When you were baptized, the preacher prophesized that you would see adversity in your life, but out of it, you would grow to be a strong woman of God.

Linda looked puzzled, and Judy said, "Andrew is scowling because we had been talking about that prophecy. When they snapped the picture, he was saying he would never let anything harm you. I remember it like it was yesterday."

They were silent a moment before Judy said what Linda was thinking, "And that very day you were taken from us."

"Do you think it was meant to be then?" Linda asked.

"I think there's a whole lot we don't understand," Judy said, "and maybe we're not even supposed to. But I do know that you've seen a lot of adversity in your life."

"So the first part came true," Linda said thoughtfully.

"And now the second part can come true too," Judy finished.

"Really?" Linda asked.

"Absolutely," Judy said. "The only difference between people who grow from adversity and those who don't is their reaction to it."

"Like what reaction?" Linda asked.

"Like letting what's happened in the past control your thoughts and actions, making your future miserable too," Judy said. "Like closing up your heart and feeling unworthy or undeserving of any good that comes to you. Andrew and I were very fortunate to have the parents and upbringing we had. You missed that. But there's no reason why you can't have that from now on. We can help you."

"Really?" Linda repeated.

"Really," Judy said, giving her another hug. "Believe it or not, you're supposed to be happy in this life. I don't think you know that. Or you push it away thinking you don't deserve it."

That's pretty true, Linda thought. "But how do I feel differently than how I feel?" she asked.

"It will take some time," Judy admitted. "But for now, just open your heart a little and let us love you and indulge us our celebration," she smiled. "Why don't you rest a little and get freshened up. Come downstairs whenever you're ready."

Judy stood up to take her leave and Linda impulsively gave her a hug. "You're the best," she said.

"Yeah?" Judy asked, smiling. "I think you just might learn to like us if you give us a chance."

Laughing, Linda said, "I already do like you!"

Before she left, Judy said, "Our goal is that you will eventually feel as entitled as Hank and Ali do."

Linda smiled at the door Judy had closed behind her. *Now there's a concept*, she thought, going to the window and looking out over the immense back yard and the majestic river beyond. It was even more beautiful than the front of the house. Chris and Chuck were coming out of the guest cottage. They walked up the snowy path to the house, holding hands and laughing. *What a cute couple they are*, she thought again. She was sorry that Jake hadn't come with her. How would she ever be able to explain all this to him? She could almost hear what he would have to say, and realized that his voice sounded a lot like the negative voice of her mother, whom she continuously argued with in her head. Was she being stupid for trying to believe that she could be a part of this family?

She shook her head in frustration and decided maybe a shower would drown out the voices that threatened to destroy her budding optimism.

Chapter Sixteen

Linda heard the doorbell ring as she came out of her bedroom. She felt nervous butterflies in her stomach at the thought of meeting so many new people tonight. Descending the stairs, she saw Andrew talking with an imposing-looking man who dominated the front hallway. Andrew was speaking quietly and seriously, and as much as she didn't want to eavesdrop, she felt a foreboding about their demeanor. She caught the words, 'phone calls,' and realized there was more to that call than Andrew had let on. *I wonder who this man is and why Andrew is telling him things he won't tell the family*, she thought, just as Andrew caught sight of her and exclaimed, "Here's my daughter now. Georgi, I'd like you to meet Captain Les McGinty."

They shook hands while Andrew explained that Les was the detective in charge of her kidnapping case.

"I just had to come and see for myself that you are alive and well," Les said. "I'm so pleased to finally meet you, Miss Lexington. You've become somewhat of a celebrity in the police department."

"Now Les," Andrew said sternly. "We're going to keep this under wraps for the time being. Georgi's got enough to handle right now."

"Oh I understand," Les said.

"Why? What would happen?" Linda asked.

"This town will probably want to put you in a parade." Les laughed. "You were a hard little lady to find."

"Yes, and the media will have a field day," Andrew said. When he noticed her anxious eyes darting between them, he said, "But we're not going to let that happen until you've had some time to adjust." He looked to Les for confirmation.

"I can't hold them off forever, Andrew," Les warned. "Somebody gets wind of this and it will be my hide."

"Nobody is going to hear about this until we're ready." Andrew said, putting a protective arm around Linda's shoulders.

"I'll do what I can," Les said. "You know I'm up for Chief this year. Closing this case would seal the deal for me." Taking Linda's hand in his again, Les said, "But you take your time, Miss Lexington, and I'll do my best to keep the vultures at bay."

Shaking Andrew's hand and preparing to leave, he said, "You enjoy your homecoming celebration, Miss Lexington. I'll talk to you next week, Andrew."

After Andrew shut the door behind Les, he said, "Come on, honey. I want to show you something before everyone gets here." He led her into the kitchen, which was bustling with activity.

"Who was at the door?" Judy asked. She was polishing silver with Hank and Ali.

Mae was supervising Chris, who was taking something out of the oven. Turning to her, Chris said, "Look Linda, Mae is showing me how to make Crème Brule!"

"Wow, I don't even know what that is," Linda laughed.

"Then you're going to have a treat tonight," Mae said, taking the pan out of Chris' hands and setting it on a hotplate.

Andrew answered Judy, saying Les had stopped by, just as John walked into the kitchen and asked, "Les was here?"

"He was anxious to meet Georgi," Andrew explained, "and I think just as anxious to close this case. Don't worry," he said to Judy's raised brows, "he said he'd hold them off for a while."

"I'm sure he'll do what he can," John said to his wife. "We've got our own little mouths to worry about."

"Who?" Hank asked, picking up on his father's subtle reference to him and Ali. Ali looked between Hank and her father, feeling that she had missed something.

Andrew said, "Speaking of secrets, let's show Georgi her surprise."

"Yay!" Ali screamed, jumping to her feet.

"Oh good, I can't wait to see your face," Chris said to Linda.

"You know about this too?" she laughed, as she was being led past the back staircase and through the door to the mud room.

Chris called out to her husband, "Come on Chuck, we're showing Linda her surprise."

Andrew held open the door leading to the garage and Ali ran out ahead of Linda, pointing to a white Jeep Wrangler with a tan top. "It's for you! Do you like it?"

Linda stood speechless on the threshold, gaping at the car.

"Well go on," Mae said from behind her, "It's not going to bite you."

Linda looked at Andrew, who was grinning at her. He shrugged and said, "Well, you said you didn't have a car."

She looked at Chris, who must have told Andrew she dreamed of having a white Jeep Wrangler. Chris was beaming too and said, "Well go on, silly. Sit in it."

Hank, patience spent, pushed past Linda and ran to open the Jeep's door. "Look, it's a stick shift."

Linda surprised everyone by bursting into tears.

"What's the matter, honey," Andrew said nervously, "Don't you like it?"

"Of course she likes it, Drew," Judy laughed. "You've just surprised the heck out of her."

"It's beautiful," Linda blubbered. She put her hand on the car, as if to make sure it wasn't a figment of her imagination. Turning to Andrew she said, "But you shouldn't, it's too much."

Andrew regained his grin and looked into her tear-filled eyes. "I've missed twenty-three Christmases and birthdays. The way I see it, I still owe you lots more presents."

She put her arms around his neck and hugged him. "Thank you," was all she managed to squeak out.

"Why don't you go sit in it so we can take your picture," John said, raising his camera.

"Here, cry baby," Chris said, handing Linda a tissue. "Wipe the mascara off your face first."

With shaky hands, Linda wiped at her face while Hank and Ali scrambled into the Jeep's back seat to get their pictures taken too. She climbed in and ran her hand lovingly over the steering wheel and dashboard. "This is what I've always wanted," she said to Andrew, and gave a big teary smile to him and the camera.

"Can we go for a ride, Uncle Andrew?" Ali asked.

"Sure we can," Andrew said, coming around to get in the passenger seat.

"Y'all don't go too far," Mae called out. Dinner will be ready in about an hour.

~ ~ ~ ~

When they pulled back into the driveway, Hank and Ali exclaimed, "Grandma and Grandpa are here!"

"Your parents?" Linda asked, parking the car with relief that she had brought everyone back safe and sound.

"No," Andrew said. "Frank and Louise are your mother's parents. They live just up the hill. My parents both died in a car accident before you were born."

The children ran into the house to greet their grandparents and Linda said, "You were an orphan too?"

"Yes, but I had a lot of family around to support me, like Frank and Louise. I don't know what I would have done without them."

They were coming into the mud room and Andrew had to shout his last words above the commotion in the kitchen. Linda pasted a nervous smile on her face and entered. Hank was proudly telling everyone that he had to tell Georgi when it was time to shift and she only stalled the new car twice.

Linda saw an older couple, both with silver hair, taking in Hank's every word as gospel and congratulating him on a job well done. Ali grabbed Linda's hand and led her to them, saying, "Grandma and Grandpa, this is Georgi."

Their seasoned faces creased in smiles and Louise came to her with arms outstretched and tears in her eyes. "Oh look, Frank, our little girl is all grown up." She pulled Linda into a hug that was surprisingly strong coming from the thin woman. Then backing up and looking at Linda fully, she said proudly, "You look just like your mama, sweetheart."

"Personally, I think she looks more like our boy, Andrew," Frank said, clasping Andrew's hand in a shake.

"She looks like Georgi," Mae said protectively. Frank gave Linda a hug and said, "Mae's right, but I must say that you're a sight for sore eyes young lady. We've waited a long time for this day."

Ted and Denise arrived then, which necessitated another round of introductions. "As you can see by our color, we're from Mae's side of the family," Ted joked.

Denise said, "We dropped everything when we heard you were coming, Georgi. We just had to see you for ourselves. It's so hard to believe...after all these years!"

Linda was introducing Chris and Chuck to everyone as Robert and Laura arrived and made their way into the chaos of the kitchen. After getting everyone's coats, Andrew said, "Why don't we go into the dining room for a toast? Mae has some superb appetizers and I have some champagne on ice."

Linda said to her Uncle Robbie and Aunt Laura, "I'm glad you're here. It's so good to see familiar faces." Looking around her, she said, "This is all so unreal, isn't it?"

"It sure is," Robert said. "Like I told you on the phone, it was as much a shock to me as it was to you. How are you holding up?"

"Good," Linda said, surprised by her own answer. "I mean, they're such wonderful people. It's been one surprise after another," she laughed.

"Well you look happy," Aunt Laura said. "Doesn't she, Robbie?"

Thinking he had never seen Linda looking so brightly animated, he said, "You look absolutely radiant tonight, Linda. Or should I call you Georgi?"

Chuck came by with a tray of champagne flutes and handed them each one. "I'd be radiant too if Andrew had just bought me a new car," he laughed good-naturedly.

Andrew raised his voice over the din to yell out to the kitchen, "Mae, Chris, come in here a minute so we can have a toast."

They did as they were told, with Mae sputtering about the dinner they were trying to prepare. They all mimicked Andrew and raised their glasses as he said, "To my daughter's miraculous return home!" There were a few "Bravos" and they all took a sip, after which Andrew raised his glass again and continued, "And to the family she's brought with her who now join ours."

"I'll drink to that," Chuck called out, as they laughed and sipped again.

Andrew wasn't finished. He raised his glass a third time and said, "And to your future, Georgi. May it surpass all of your expectations and fulfill all your hopes and dreams."

As Mae turned to go back to the kitchen, Judy said, "One more toast."

"One more sip and I won't care about dinner anymore," Mae said with an uncharacteristic giggle.

"Neither will the rest of us," Frank laughed.

Judy put a hand on Mae's arm to arrest her retreat. Raising her glass, she said, "And may you find the Georgi within you, the woman you were born to be."

"Spoken like a true analyst, my dear," John teased, while everyone, except Linda, laughed. *That's exactly what I need*, she thought. What was the word Judy had used earlier? Entitled? Oh how she wanted to feel entitled to these wonderful people's love! She looked around at the Lexingtons. Judy was happy and fulfilled. Andrew was brave and loving. The children were secure in knowing their rightful place in the world.

And then she noticed something else. They were all looking at her, waiting for some type of response. Maybe it was the champagne, or the heady blush of her heart opening, but whatever gave her the courage, she spoke with all the sincerity she possessed.   "Thank you all for being so wonderful. I want to be a part of this family."

As if they had been waiting for her acceptance, Andrew shouted, "Here, here! Its official, let the party begin! Caught up in a pandemonium of tears and hugs and basking in the glow of love and acceptance unlike anything she had ever known, she hugged Chris and told her she loved her, which was the first time she could remember ever doing that with her sister.

Much later as she lay in bed re-living the unforgettable evening, she snuggled into her cocoon of blankets, happy and content with the expectation of waking to emerge from that cocoon a butterfly, free from the torment of her past and able to fly on the updraft of the love she felt in this house.

Instead, she awoke with a start a while later, struggling to break free of the confining, suffocating blankets that felt as if they were burying her alive.   Heart pounding and sweating profusely, she finally tore free and sat up, disoriented and terrified. The nightmare was so vivid that she still thought she was in her father Mike's house, until she calmed down enough to realize she was in Andrew's house.

In her dream, she had gone to visit Mike. When she got there, he had another little daughter, probably about five or six years old (who looked a lot like her when she was that age, she thought).   But this little girl was insistent on getting and keeping her father's attention and wouldn't let them talk. Linda finally said to her father, *I haven't seen you in so many years and I really want to talk to you. Will you please talk to me?*

He said, *Sure*, and just as calmly as could be, raised a gun and shot the little girl in the head. Then, as dreams sometimes go, her mother was standing in front of her. She tried to tell her what her father had done, but her mother wouldn't believe her, so Linda took her out back to the garbage can to show her the evidence. She took the lid off and pushed aside the garbage on top to show her mother that her father had installed a meat grinder in there and was grinding up the evidence of his crime. Her mother still wouldn't believe her, so Linda took hold of the handle to the meat grinder and started turning. With a partial turn of the handle, however, she realized two things simultaneously: that she was now implicated in his crime and would be punished along with him, and that she was the girl in the garbage can. She screamed in pain at what her own hand was doing to herself.

With shaking hands and weak legs, she got out of bed and reached for the light. *It was just a dream*, she told herself. But if it was just a dream, how could she smell the garbage on her? The stench was so pervasive and sickening, she had to run into the bathroom to throw up. Trying to be quiet so as not to wake Ali, she retched until all that was left in her were dry heaves. Finally finished, she pulled on some clothes over her pajamas and reached with trembling hands into her purse for her cigarettes.   As quietly as she could, she made her way downstairs and out to the garage to sneak a smoke.

Turning the light on in the garage, her eyes were dazzled by the shiny new Jeep sitting there waiting for her. A strong sense of relief swept through her. She had somehow expected this physical evidence of Andrew's love to have rolled off on its own into the dark night. But no, here it was, as ignorant of her guilt and inadequacy as Andrew was.

Just as she was lighting her cigarette, the door to the house opened and John peered out.

"I thought I heard something," he said, as he stepped out into the garage. "Am I interrupting your love affair with your new car or that cigarette you're hiding behind your back?"

"Both, I guess," she said sheepishly. "I'm sorry I woke you."

"Who me? I'm a night owl. Mind if I join you?"

She shook her head and looked at him in amazement as he took two folding chairs off a hook on the wall, and cracked open a window. "Have a seat," he said, and disappeared back into the house, reappearing moments later with a cigar and two glasses of cognac. Handing her one of the glasses, he dropped the tailgate of the truck parked beside her Jeep and sat down in a chair, propping his feet up on the tailgate, and releasing an "Ahhhhh" as he settled in. "Judy hates it when I smoke a cigar," he said, lighting up. "But I'd say this is a special occasion," winking at her. "Sit down and relax."

"You're not angry?" she asked, finally finding her voice and sitting down next to him.

"Angry about what?" he asked. "Last I checked, we were both over twenty-one and free," he grinned.

She laughed, liking his easy-going, teasing manner.

"Besides," he said, "it gives us a chance to get to know each other apart from all the hoopla."

"Hoopla?" she laughed again.

"Yeah, Andrew and I are pretty much workaholics, but the older I get, the more I like to just sit back and enjoy a nice cigar and some quiet music in my free time and I don't care much for having a bunch of people around. That's why I love Florida. We could be sitting on the beach right now enjoying the sound of the ocean. I hope you're going with us."

"Oh, I don't know…"

"That whole thing about you coming to babysit was just a ruse, you know."

"It's not that," she said. "I'd like to come, but my boyfriend, well, he's not very happy that I'm here. He's jealous, or threatened, by Andrew, I think."

"Sounds to me like you need a new boyfriend," John said matter-of-factly.

"It's not that easy," she mused.

"Sure it is, sweetheart," he grinned. "You just live your life and be happy and you'll have all kinds of men begging to be a part of it."

"I wish you were right," she said, "but…"

"I am right," he declared. "You're young and beautiful, and you don't need to blush like that, it's the truth. Hell, Judy and I didn't get married until we were in our thirties."

"How did you meet her?" she asked.

"Andrew and I were college roommates. I met Judy when I came home with him that first Thanksgiving. She was seventeen. I carried a secret crush on her for years but she never saw me that way. She just thought I was some playboy jokester, which I guess is what it looked like. But the truth is, I dated around a lot because I just couldn't find anyone who could hold a candle to her."

"That's sweet," she said.

Laughing, he said, "It wasn't so sweet at the time. In fact, it was downright frustrating. She looked past me like I wasn't even there. She was busy with her friends and her school and her family – she is so full of life and purpose. I've always admired that about her."

"So you weren't jealous or threatened by that?" she asked.

"Jealous, for sure. But not threatened. I didn't want her to change. I just wanted to be a part of her life."

"Jake's not trying to change me, he just feels threatened by Andrew for some reason."

John looked at her with half a smile and said, "All I know is that if I ever tried to prevent Judy from being with her family or friends or anyone else, for that matter, she would leave me in a cloud of dust so fast my head would spin. I'd probably have a sore jaw to boot," he laughed. Getting serious again, he said, "Domination comes in many forms, sweetheart."

"Domination," she said, trying the word on to see if it fit.

"I mean the dominating kind of love where they force you to do something against your wishes or better judgment because they love you so much and they know what's best for you."

Linda gave a little gasp, feeling the "click" of the fit. "Jake *does* love me," she protested meekly.

"I'm sure he does, sweetheart," John replied quickly. "I'm just saying some people love differently than other people. But if things don't add up right and you ignore the signs, it's like not balancing your checkbook because you're afraid you've run out of money."

They heard the door to the house open and both turned around to see Andrew, hooding his eyes with his hand and squinting from the garage light. "I thought I heard voices out here," he said, coming over to stand beside Georgi. "What's the matter, honey, couldn't you sleep?"

"I had a bad dream," she said sheepishly, stubbing out her cigarette.

"Oh sweetie," Andrew said, taking her hand to pull her up in a hug. "You're…"

The gunshots came from the window one second before Judy's scream from the threshold of the house. Andrew and Georgi crumpled slowly to the floor, falling in slow motion through time and space into complete darkness.

Chapter Seventeen

"Sweetheart, why don't you go get something to eat? I'll watch over Andrew until you get back." Georgi was keeping vigil over a sleeping Andrew; her back half sitting on the hospital chair and her front half resting on the bed.

Through red and swollen eyes, Georgi looked up and asked Judy, "How's John?"

"He's stable. The doctor says he'll be fine, though. It's Drew here that I'm worried about," Judy said, kissing Andrew's forehead.

"What are you worried about, Sis?" Andrew moaned, before opening his eyes.

The two women pivoted to look, unsure they had indeed heard words coming out of the motionless body. Judy, snapping out of her shock, buzzed frantically for the nurse, "It's you I'm worried about, Drew, you've given us quite a scare."

Andrew gingerly turned his head toward her voice, "How's Georgi? he croaked. "Is she okay?"

"I'm right here, Dad," Georgi said through a stream of tears. Taking his hand and squeezing it in confirmation, she said, "I was afraid I was going to lose you."

The effort of moving and talking brought on a coughing spell.

"It's okay, Drew," Judy said soothingly. "Sssshhhh, just be still and take it easy. Everybody is okay."

"John?" Andrew wheezed.

"He's going to be fine. Just relax, okay?"

"What happened?" he moaned, as the nurse who had responded to Judy's call blazed a flashlight into his eyes.

"They can tell you all about it in a few minutes," said the skinny nurse wearing platform shoes and an attitude. "Right now, though, they're going to go to the waiting room while we examine you." She leveled an ominous gaze at the women. Georgi gave Andrew's hand another quick squeeze.

"We'll be right back, Drew," Judy told him, turning to go, but not before volleying a glare of her own back at the nurse.

Newspaper reporters were swarming the hospital lobby, trying to get news on Andrew's condition and to find out if the rumors of Georgi's return were true. To keep them from being exposed to the barrage, the two women were ushered into a private office off the surgical wing where Andrew and John had been rushed the night before. John had a bullet in his left shoulder, which they were able to remove; Andrew had taken two shots to the lower back, one of them severing his spine. The surgeons had been able to remove the bullets and repair most of his intestines, but by the look on the face of the approaching doctor, the news wasn't good.

"Andrew is still in very critical condition," he said. "He's bleeding internally and although we've slowed it, we haven't been able to stop it as yet. I'm afraid he can't go on much longer like this."

With heavy hearts and forced bravado, the women returned to Andrew's room on tiptoes. He heard them come in, opened his eyes and whispered, "Tell me what happened."

Georgi asked him, "Do you remember being in the garage last night?"

"You mean when I interrupted your smoking break?" he smiled.

"Good, you do remember," Judy said. "The shots came from the window in the garage. John was hit in the shoulder but he's going to be fine."

"Do they know who did it?"

"Not yet," Judy said. "Les was here earlier to talk to you, but you were sleeping. He said something about you receiving some threatening phone calls?"

Andrew looked at Georgi, then back to Judy. "I don't know who it was and I don't want to make any accusations."

"I know you don't want a repeat of what happened when we blamed Seth," Judy said. "But what did he say?"

The effort of talking brought on another coughing spell and they tried to calm him.

"It's okay, Dad. You're going to be okay," Georgi said with more conviction than she felt. She wiped her tears with her sleeve.

Judy's tears were running down her cheeks as Andrew, now calm, said to her, "I love you Jude. Go take care of that husband of yours while I talk to Georgi, okay?"

Judy leaned over him, wetting his cheek with her tears as she kissed it. "I love you too, Drew. I'll see you soon."

"Later," he smiled at her.

Turning to Georgi, he tried to raise his arm to wipe her tears, but was unable to lift it high enough to reach her face, groaning with the pain and frustration of the attempt. She lowered her head into his hand and unabashedly cried out a lifetime of sorrow and loss.

Finally raising her head to tell him she was sorry for losing it, she melted at the love in his patient eyes and again broke down, letting her sobbing face fall back into his open hand.

He used his thumb to stroke her cheek until she calmed down and could finally sputter, "I'm sorry."

He put his thumb under her chin to lift it so she had to look at him and said sternly, "I don't want you ever to apologize for how you feel." Softening, he said, "You have this pervasive guilt for having been born or taking up space on this earth. All those feelings are based on lies, Georgi."

"You're my daughter, and I love you dearly. No matter what happens," he added.

"I just want you to live," she whispered through her tears.

"You will always have me," he promised.

"How can you say that?" she cried. "After everybody in my life has left or died, and just when you've finally convinced me that I'm your daughter. . . only to come to this?"

Her voice was loud enough to summon a nurse, who rushed in to see what all the yelling was about and try to remove her from the room.

"Don't touch me!" she screamed at the nurse, defying her order to leave.

The nurse looked at Andrew in frustration, only to see a sad smile on his face. He nodded to her that it was okay and she left the room in a huff.

"It's not fair!" Georgi continued. "God is mean and cruel and teases me into loving someone, only to jerk them out of my life. It's spiteful and mean and vicious. What does He want me to do? Keep getting back on my feet just so He can knock me down again?"

"Is this funny?" she asked, because his smile had grown wider.

"No, it's not funny. I'm just happy to see that you're finally not blaming yourself for everything. I'm sure God is happy about that too and doesn't mind that you're mad at Him."

"It's not fair!" she said again, slumping, spent, onto the chair beside his bed, crying softly into the mattress.

When she later looked up, Andrew had dozed off and Georgi whispered, "Please don't leave me."

She watched his breathing carefully, wanting more than anything to look into his intense blue eyes again. What had been so uncomfortable to her previously, she was now ready to accept and embrace. Was it too late? How could she have lived her whole life not knowing she was so empty? She felt that if she could fill herself up with Andrew's love, it would squeeze out all the negative feelings she harbored about herself.

Andrew was right; her life had been based on lies. Not just about her parents, but about God too. It felt like a lead weight had suddenly been lifted off her heart and she could now see how God had orchestrated her path to this moment; to the man who had searched the world for her. The perception brought with it the realization that God, her true Father, loved her enough to seek her out and touch her heart. She suddenly knew that God would not disappoint her on this.

Judy came quietly into the room, carrying a tray of food.

"I thought maybe you could eat something," she said.

"Georgi picked her head off the bed and said, "I believe he's going to be okay, Judy!"

"I'm happy to hear you've found some hope!"

Georgi pulled Judy away from the bed so they wouldn't disturb Andrew and whispered, "You won't believe the experience I just had!"

"Looks like it was a good one," Judy smiled.

"It was like I was talking to God. With my heart. I can't explain it! But I know now that He isn't mad at me and doesn't hate me. I've always expected bad things to happen because I thought He hated me and wanted to punish me. But what He wants for me is all good! It's like He's been waiting for me to realize that and believe that!"

Together they looked at Andrew sleeping quietly and Judy said, "I do believe that God has spoken to your heart, Georgi. Let's hold on to that belief."

"In the meantime, I hate to spoil the moment, but the hospital is holding a press conference in an hour. I brought you some clean clothes and some make-up so you'll look presentable."

"Why? What does that have to do with me?" Georgi asked.

Sighing, Judy said, "They can't hold off the reporters and the people swarming the hospital forever. Everyone wants to see you. They figure the only way to calm them is to have you go out there and say hello and let them get their pictures. Don't be afraid. I'll be right beside you."

Standing in the shower, Georgi felt as if she were washing away years, rather than hours, of dirt, sweat and tears. She'd heard people say, 'change your thoughts, change your life,' but she had never understood the concept. The switch from, '*God hates me*,' to '*God loves me*,' however, changed everything. *It's more than a thought, really, that Andrew could live. I feel it in my heart. Am I going crazy now on top of everything else?* she wondered. *Or am I just setting myself up to be disappointed?*

"You look like a new woman," Judy remarked when Georgi came out of the bathroom.

"I feel like one!" Georgi smiled. How's Dad doing?

Judy was standing by Andrew, stroking his hair. "He's sleeping peacefully."

"I'm so hungry all of a sudden!" Georgi said, digging into the food Judy had brought.

"So tell me about this experience you had," Judy said. "It sounds wonderful."

"It was. And confusing. I don't know how to explain it. I hear my mother's voice in my head all the time, but this was different. This was in my heart. I'm not sure if I'm hearing it right. Am I setting myself up for disappointment if I allow myself to believe that he will live?"

Judy came and sat down beside her. "I think you're so used to thinking and preparing for the worst that you're having a hard time believing anything positive. My dad, your granddad, used to say that we will have many enemies in our lives, but doubt will hurt us more than anyone else ever can. You doubt God, then you doubt yourself, and then you start thinking you're crazy."

Laughing, Georgi said, "Yes! That's exactly how I feel. Like there is a battle going on in my head and new thoughts like *God doesn't hate me* challenge everything I've ever known. If I could really believe that, it changes everything....what I think about myself, the whole world for that matter."

"I'm so happy that you've had that revelation," Judy said. "Although it's the beginning of some tough battles for you, I hate to say. Your mind is going to play some pretty mean tricks on you to keep control of the way you've always thought about yourself, but I'll help you through it."

There was a knock on the door and a nurse poked her head around to say that there was an urgent call for Linda Bigelow from Jake Kingsley. "I told him there was no one here by that name, but he keeps calling back and now insists on talking to you, Georgi."

Georgi looked at Judy in a panic. "I don't know what to say to him. He's going to be so mad at me."

Always the practical one, Judy said, "You need to get ready for the press conference right now. Why don't you take some time and get your thoughts together and decide how you want to handle this?"

Georgi looked over at the sleeping Andrew; remembering his words about never having to apologize for her feelings. Turning to the nurse, she said, "Please tell Jake that I'm not able to talk right now but I'll call him tomorrow."

Les McGinty was right behind the retreating nurse and announced that it was time to go downstairs and talk to the press.

Standing up, Judy held out her hand, "Are you ready?"

As Les escorted them to the lobby, Judy inquired about the investigation.

"We'll talk after the press conference," Les said. "Wait here in the lobby for now until the Mayor finishes his speech. I'll be back to accompany you out to the podium."

"The Mayor of Pittsburgh is out there?" Georgi gasped. She tightened her grip on Judy's hand, looking at her with terror in her eyes.

"It's okay, honey," Judy said. "He's just a man like everybody else. You just remember who *you* are."

As if in a dream, she was standing in front of hundreds of people who were taking pictures of her and straining to get a better look. They were happy and excited - some even crying! She realized that they were clapping their hands for *her* and yelling for her to speak.

"Hello," she said, feeling silly. Judy squeezed her hand and she got bolder.

"I'm Georgia Lexington."

The crowd went wild with applause! When it died down, she continued. "I'm happy to be home. Thank you for all your support."

Someone yelled out, "How's Andrew?"

"My father is alive!" she answered.

When the cheers and applause subsided, she continued, "He never gave up hope of finding me. He's given me his faith, love and courage and I won't give up hope on him now."

Chapter Eighteen

"I didn't want to say anything before," Les said to Judy and Georgi after the press conference, "because I didn't want to rattle you, but before you came out to the podium, we made an announcement that we captured the person who shot John and Andrew."

"Who was it?" they asked in unison.

"It was Seth McPherson. I know your question," he continued before they could ask, "and the answer is that he escaped prison day before yesterday. Apparently he faked an illness convincingly enough to be taken to the hospital, and from there he walked right past the guard at his door after he knocked out and took the doctor's scrubs. We put out an all-points bulletin for his arrest and grabbed him yesterday."

"I can't believe it!" Judy exclaimed. "Has he confessed? Are you sure he did it?"

"Yes," Les said. "He didn't put up any resistance and he's made a full confession. Apparently the only goal left in his life was to make Andrew pay. Let's hope he hasn't succeeded."

Judy thanked Les and told him she would tell Andrew. But when they arrived back at Andrew's room, they found his doctor, wearing a concerned frown, waiting for them in the hall.

"Is Andrew okay?" Judy asked anxiously.

"I'm afraid that Andrew has slipped into a coma," he replied. Responding to their terrified expressions, he belatedly tried to soften the blow. "This isn't unusual, it's the body's way of dealing with the trauma."

"Does this mean he's getting worse?" Georgi asked.

"I had hoped this wouldn't happen," the doctor admitted reluctantly. "Only time will tell."

"How much time?" Judy asked.

"I don't know, it could be hours or it could be days." Speaking to Judy, he said, "John, on the other hand, is doing just fine and I'm releasing him. Why don't you both take him home and get some rest? We'll call you if there is any change with Andrew."

Judy thanked the doctor and turned to a morose and silent Georgi. "Remember what I said about your belief being tested? Well, this is it. Don't give up on Andrew now."

"I won't. You're right."

"Let's go home and get some rest. We can be back here in a matter of minutes when Andrew wakes up."

"Thanks, no. I want to be here."

~ ~ ~ ~

"Hi Dad, it's me, Georgi," she said to Andrew after Judy had kissed him goodbye. She didn't know if he could hear her or not, but she needed to believe that he could.

"You won't believe what just happened," she said to his silence. "They held a press conference - about me! I had to stand in front of all those people and cameras and tell them who I was and that you had found me." Wistfully, she said, "It may sound weird, but I loved the pride I felt for a second out there on the podium, when I could lift my chin and say that my name is Georgia Lexington. It's so much more than a name, really, or even the history of your name." She sat down next to Andrew's bed, her head buried deep in thought. "It's the fact that Georgia Lexington was born to be loved. The little girl in the picture you showed me was passed around and shown off with pride. She had a bright future because she was loved and cherished. I sure don't feel like that little girl.....not even close."

Silently, she reminisced, *No matter how hard I tried, it was never good enough. I could never do enough.* She could still hear her mother's voice, repeating her often-asked question, *"Who do you think you are?"* The implied answer to that question being, *"Nobody."*

She wondered how many people in the world wished they had been born to different parents; loving, kind parents like Andrew and his wife. All the facts said she *had* been born to those parents, yet, she couldn't wrap her mind around the fact that she was born to be loved and adored. You can't take for granted what you've never had, she was learning.

Facts were one thing. What her mind was telling her was another. Right now it was saying, *boo hoo – you had it so rough and all that time you were meant to be treated like a princess – right! What makes you so special?*

Her self-pitying thoughts were interrupted when the door to the room flew open and a nurse rushed in, apologizing for intruding but brushed aside by Jake, who strode purposefully in behind her. Sneering contemptuously at the nurse, he said to Georgi, "No one will let me talk to you. I had to drive all the way from Cleveland just to see if you were still alive."

Stunned and temporarily confused, Georgi stammered, "Alive? Why of course . . oh, the shooting." It seemed weeks ago the shots had cracked through the still night.

"Yes, it's okay," she said to the nurse, in answer to her question. "I know him."

Taking Georgi into his arms, Jake said, "I've been so worried about you, Linda. I called and called, but they wouldn't put me through."

"Didn't you see the interview on TV?" Georgi asked.

"What interview? I've been driving for hours. I told you it was a bad idea to come here, Linda."

"Oh, Jake, I'm so sorry!" She hugged him tight.

"Well, I'm glad you're all right," he said, softening. Taking her hand in his, "Now will you listen to me? Come on, let's go home."

"Home? Jake, I can't go home right now! Andrew is in a coma and fighting for his life!"

With hardening eyes, Jake dropped Georgi's hand in a display of dismissal. In the tone of talking to a child, he said, "I've had enough of this nonsense, Linda. I can't believe you would throw away our relationship over this man."

"Throw away? No! Jake, I love you!"

"You sure have a strange way of showing it," he snarled. "In fact, what you're showing me is that you don't care about me at all." He turned to go, hesitated, and then added, "You have a choice to make, Linda."

Throwing herself at him, she begged, "Please Jake, just listen to me. Let me explain."

"I'm waiting."

Georgi pulled herself up in a show of strength Jake had never before seen in her and said, "It's all true, Jake. I really am Andrew's daughter who was kidnapped." Stopping him from interrupting, she said, "Please, just let me finish. It seems to me that you're the one who doesn't care enough to find out the truth about me. Andrew is my father. He has spent half his life looking for me. He was standing in front of me when the bullets hit him in the back. I can't leave him now, nor can I go back to being Linda Bigelow. I'm just beginning to discover who I really am, and I hoped that you would want to be with me through this."

"Well, we have a problem, then, *Linda*, because I fell in love with Linda Bigelow. I don't even recognize you right now."

"You don't understand," she tried again.

"I'll tell you what I *do* understand. What happens when he dies and you're left with nobody? You can't make it on your own, Linda. I also understand that you are not one of *them*," he spat contemptuously at Andrew.

"Why are you making me choose like this, Jake? And what do you mean, 'one of them?'"

"These people are putting crazy ideas in your head, Linda. This isn't you talking, this is them talking."

"You're wrong, Jake. What they've shown me is what it feels like to be loved, and right now, you're not acting like you love me. How can you make me choose between them and you?"

"Who are you? You're talking like a spoiled brat Lexington!"

Jake opened the door, leaving his parting words to simmer in his wake. "I'm the best you've ever had, Linda. You're going to regret your decision."

"Jake, wait...." but she was talking to a closed door.

Confused and alone, she began to think that maybe Jake was right. What if Andrew died and she was left alone? And now without a job because she had not called to tell them why she was still in Pittsburgh. Yet, she couldn't bring herself to run after Jake. She felt like she was sitting on a fence, unable to go back, but also unable to go forward.

No, dammit! She scolded herself. *I know I've done the right thing by staying here with Andrew. I'm done being manipulated by Jake's anger and I'm not going to feel guilty for making him mad!*

She knew instinctively this wasn't about security or her job. This was about love. Before she met Andrew or Judy, or ever heard the name Lexington, she thought love was about pleasing people. She had never experienced love for being just who she was; even if she was being a brat, as Jake had said. She thought about how rude she had been to Andrew; she thought about how she could say anything on her mind to Judy. They loved her no matter what she did or said to them just because she was who she was.

She must have dozed off, because she woke with a start when Judy asked, "Are you okay? They called to tell me Jake was here and left in a very dark mood."

Grinning, Georgi said, "I thought you could read my mind. I was just thinking about you."

Taking her coat off and placing a covered dish on the nightstand, Judy said, "Mae sent you some dinner. So what happened?"

Sighing, Georgi said, "Oh Judy, I can't figure out if I'm the one who's changed all that much or if it's Jake who's so different. He used to listen to me like he was really trying to get to know me and cared what I thought. Now he won't listen to me unless I do what he wants me to do."

"Let me guess," Judy said. "He wants you to go home with him and forget you're a Lexington. He wants to go back to the time when you were sweet little Linda Bigelow who had no agenda of her own."

"Exactly. I just don't understand. I thought he cared about me."

"He does, in his own way. He's threatened by all this, by the change in you. He's not in control of you anymore."

"John said something like that. He said he'd never be able to control you or you'd leave him coughing in the dust." Laughing, Georgi added, "How is John, by the way?"

"He'll be back to his fine self in no time," Judy assured her. "He's a gem, all right. He respects me. I guess it comes down to that. But Georgi, *you're* the one who tells a person how to treat you – not by your words so much as your confidence; your attitude. What you will or will not accept."

"I just want him to love me like he used to," she whined.

Silently assessing her for a minute, Judy said, "I have to tell you I'm very proud that you stood your ground with him."

"Really?" Georgi gave a mournful smile.

"Yes, really. I know you want love and you'll do just about anything to get it, even disregard what you want or change who you are, but that is not real love, Georgi. It will last only as long as you're able to ignore your own needs."

"But isn't that selfish? If I love him, shouldn't I want to please him? Shouldn't I want to do what he wants?"

"To an extent," Judy answered, "if we're talking about getting him a muffin," she laughed. But seriously, there are compromises and give-and-take in every relationship. I'm not talking about that. I'm talking about him respecting you enough to let you make your own decisions. Let's talk about why you love him."

"Oh, that's easy," Georgi said. "Because of the way he made me feel; the way he loved me. It's sad to be talking about it like it's in the past. That's what I want back more than anything. It's almost like I can't love myself or feel worthy of love unless he loves me like that," she mussed.

"That's a very astute observation," Judy said. "Most people can't see that and continually try to make other people fill the loveless hole in their heart. People with holes in their heart just keep hurting each other through no intention of their own. They're just trying to fill the hole."

Judy saw Georgi's questioning look and continued, "That's what Jake is trying to do, too. He feels you love him if you're doing what he says and what he wants. Otherwise he feels unloved and alone too. If he had a healthy self-esteem, he wouldn't feel so threatened."

"And if I had a healthy self-esteem?" she asked.

"Then you would be loving a man who respects you and your needs."

Georgi groaned. "But how can you help who you love?"

"You can't," Judy said simply. "We're all magnets and we attract those people who are most like us. That is, we attract people with pretty much the same size hole in their heart as ours."

Judy thought she heard Georgi groan again, but Georgi was looking at Andrew, who was turning his head and moaning.

"He's awake!" she yelled.

The girls scrambled to get on opposite sides of Andrew's bed. Georgi was crying unabashed tears of joy as Judy reached for the nurse's call button.

"Not yet, Jude," Andrew said, stopping her arm in its pursuit.

"How are you feeling?" Georgi wept.

"Better than you can imagine," Andrew said. He had opened his eyes and they were luminous. "I have so much to tell you."

Concerned, Judy said, "Just take it easy, Drew. Let's get the doctor in here to check you out. Are you in pain?"

"No," Andrew said. "I need to tell you before it goes away."

"What goes away?" Judy asked. "A dream?"

Shaking his head slowly, Andrew said, "It wasn't a dream. It was so real. I could see Georgi sitting here by the bed as I floated up. She was getting smaller and smaller. Then I was in a different place altogether."

"Was it heaven?" Georgi asked, spellbound.

Andrew thought about the question carefully. "I guess so, but...."

Judy interrupted him, "Oh my God, Andrew. I'm so glad they sent you back to us!"

"It wasn't like that," he said. "I chose to come back. I didn't see God, but I *felt* Him."

"What was it like?" Georgi asked.

"So hard to put into words," he said pensively. "It's easier to say what it *wasn't*. I had no fear – of anything! I've never felt anything like it! No fear and no worries; like all that was left down here."

"Wow," Georgi said. "I can't even imagine."

"It was the lightest, yet most powerful, feeling in the world! I was truly a part of this astronomical creation; I've never felt more confident and bold and free."

He closed his eyes and on his face was an expression that said he wanted to hold on to the feeling and not let it drift away.

Concerned he would be lost to them again, Judy startled him alert with the announcement that she was going to get the doctor. On her way out the door, she instructed Georgi to keep Andrew awake while she was gone.

Andrew took Georgi's hand. "If I don't do anything else with the rest of my life, I want to show you that power of knowing who you really are and where you came from. That's why I came back."

"I'm beginning to realize that I'm a Lexington," Georgi laughed nervously. He was scaring her with his intensity.

"Being a Lexington or a Bigelow has nothing to do with what I just saw. Everything we've learned, everything we've ever known, is just a tiny piece of the puzzle; and not such a good piece, either, because we're taught from the time we're little to fear everything. I didn't think I had a lot of fear in me until I felt what it was like to be without it!"

"I had a boldness I've never felt before, and, boy, is it exhilarating! It wasn't like I *felt* I could do anything, I *knew* I could. I was totally safe, knowing nothing could hurt me because I had the power of the universe backing me up. For the first time, I know who I really am and where I came from, and it's not just the Lexington family. We were conceived in the belly of the universe; born endowed with the power of creation and the wisdom of the ages. Yet, a very dark force here conspires to make us forget that the minute we're born."

Judy came back with the doctor and his entourage, who then asked them to leave so they could examine Andrew.

As they were leaving, Andrew called out, "Don't you see, Georgi? That's why we're here. Everything that's happened has brought us to this point of finding out who we really are."

In the hall, Judy said, "Fill me in, what did he say while I was gone?"

"I'm not really sure, but he kind of scared me. I hope he hasn't gone crazy or something."

"He didn't sound crazy to me," Judy said. "I kind of envy him the experience."

"Yes, but after you left he was saying some weird things, like there's a vast conspiracy in this world to keep us from our power; or things like if we really knew who we were, we would be all powerful or something, kind of like God!"

Judy was thoughtful for a moment. "That does sound kind of crazy, but let's give him the benefit of the doubt and hear him out. Andrew is the last person to have a God complex and he's not one for dramatics. I don't doubt he had an out-of-this-world experience, but he's back in reality now and maybe he'll be able to explain it to us."

"It was so unlike him, at least as far as I know him."

"Let's just keep an open mind," Judy said. "There's so much about this world we don't know or understand."

The doctor came out to inform them that, for Andrew's own safety, they had to sedate him. "He became extremely agitated when we wouldn't let him get out of bed and walk. He insisted that he could."

"Will his spine heal?" Judy asked. "Will he ever walk again?"

"Maybe one day, but it will take surgery, therapy, prayer and a lot of time. They'll be coming to get him in a little bit to take some x-rays, but you can go in now."

Looking at each other for silent support, they opened the door and entered Andrew's room. He was sleeping, and Judy used the phone by his bed to call home and tell them Andrew had come out of the coma.

Georgi went to the opposite side and took Andrew's hand in hers. He turned his head to her and opened groggy eyes.

"I wish they hadn't drugged me," he murmured.

"It's okay, Dad. Just rest now. We have our whole lives to talk. Just get better now, okay?"

Chapter Nineteen

"You're home now," Mae said, having taken dictatorial charge of the wheelchair the minute Judy pulled the car up to the house. "And none too soon, neither."

Chuckling, Andrew said, "I'm happy to see you too, Mae."

She pushed him into the kitchen while the girls unloaded the car of its cargo, most of which were flower arrangements sent to the hospital for Andrew.

Finally joining them in the kitchen, Georgi said, "I thought we gave away most of the flowers you received!"

Judy kissed Mae's cheek and asked, "Where is everybody?"

"John and the kids went into town to get some things from Andrew's apartment."

"I'm going to have his hide," Judy sputtered. "He's not supposed to be driving with one arm in a sling!"

"Then lucky for him he's not the one driving," Mae said. "Robert came over to help switch bedrooms around and then drove them into town."

"I promise I won't be needing your room for long, my Mae. I'm going to be able to climb those stairs in no time."

"Don't you worry about climbing stairs." Mae set a pot of chili on the table. "And don't you go setting yourself up for disappointment, Andrew. The doctor said it's going to be a while before you can walk again."

The wonderful smells wafting up from the pot on the table obliterated all conversation. The only sounds were spoons on bowls until Georgi blurted, "Who's that?" trying not to choke on the piece of bread she had been chewing on. She was looking out the patio window at a man walking up the path from the cottage. If she had to describe him in one word, she would have said "healthy." He wasn't handsome in the traditional sense of the word, but he had an open, friendly presence. He looked clean cut and muscular, and radiated wholesomeness.

Watching Georgi ogle him, Judy laughed. "I know you're thinking the same thing I did when I met him. That's Doug, Andrew's physical therapist. Lucky for us, he's going to be staying here a while."

Georgi shot Andrew a glance and found he wasn't very happy with the news. She had learned in the past few days how difficult it was for him to be dependent on others.

"Will you tolerate him for our sake?" she asked, trying to make him smile.

But rather than returning her smile, alarm grew in his eyes and then she heard Judy's gasp. Looking back outside, she saw that Doug was surrounded by a pack of reporters snapping his picture and asking him questions.

Judy was half off her chair, about to rescue him, when she stopped and chuckled. "He looks like he can hold his own pretty well."

True enough, he was not cowering from the mob, but rather standing tall and smiling for the cameras. He was answering some of their questions and making a statement of his own. His bold demeanor caused them to back up and give him space for his impromptu press conference.

"Very impressive!" Judy said, sitting back down. They were all staring at the scene outside when the garage door opened, followed a few seconds later by the kids running into the kitchen.

"Uncle Andrew!" they exclaimed, and climbed on his lap.

John and Robert were close behind. "Apparently we have Doug to thank for getting through all those TV trucks out front," John said, observing the scene in the back yard.

"Your timing is impeccable," Andrew said. "Will you close the blinds so we can have some privacy? The hospital said they would give us enough time to get home before they announced I had been released, but we had no idea you two were out running around town."

All heads turned to Andrew. He sounded different; his tone was jaded with the intended joke. But the moment passed and John and Robert pulled the shades down as Doug entered through the back door.

"I don't think you'll have to worry about those," he said to John. "They're leaving."

"How the heck did you get them to leave?" Judy asked, astounded.

Grinning, he said, "By promising to give them an update every day at 11:00. This way, we only have to deal with them for a half hour a day."

"Smart man," John said. "Wish I had thought of that myself!"

Ali and Hank, having already spent a day with Doug while he settled into the house and its routine, abandoned Andrew's lap for Doug, who in turn tossed them up in the air as effortlessly as if they were squealing bean bags. Setting them each solidly back on the floor, he shook Georgi's hand. "You must be the lovely Miss Georgia all those reporters were asking about."

Blushing, she took his hand, embarrassingly unable to think of a response. Undaunted, he held out his hand to Andrew, saying he was also glad to make his acquaintance.

Andrew shocked everyone by saying, "I don't need a nursemaid." When he realized how rude he had been, he apologized. "I'm sorry, I'm just very tired. I think I'll go in and lay down."

"Of course," Doug said, taking the handles of Andrew's wheelchair. "I'll help you."

Andrew put his hands on the wheels, stopping the chair's momentum. "Thanks, but no. I can do it." To everyone's astonishment, he rolled himself off toward the bedroom.

John was the first to respond. "I'll go help him," he said, rising from his chair.

"No," Judy stopped him. "Let him be for now."

~ ~ ~ ~

Hours later, Georgi knocked quietly on his door. "Andrew? . . . Dad?"

She opened it to find him lying on his back, fully clothed, staring at the ceiling.

"Are you okay?" she asked.

He raised himself up on his elbows, "I'm sorry for being such a bear out there."

"I don't blame you for being frustrated. It's just so unlike you, is all."

"Oh, Georgi," he sighed, laying back down and looking at the ceiling again. "I don't want to live like this."

"What are you saying?" she asked, panic rising in her.

Andrew rolled over on his side to face her. "Don't worry, honey. I'm not going to do anything to myself. What I mean is, this world is now so bleak compared to the world I was in."

Relieved with his explanation, she said, "Mae says you caught a glimpse of the sweet bye and bye. I guess in the meantime, you're just going to have to put up with us mortals," she joked, trying to lighten the mood.

"That's not the problem," he hastened to explain. "I know that I'm supposed to live what I discovered and teach you how to find it. But how can I do that if I can't find it again?"

"When I first woke up," he continued, "I knew that I could walk. But they wouldn't let me. They said I would irreparably damage myself. Now I'm afraid to try. But Georgi, I *knew* that I could! It was as factual as these walls are blue! I was so confident and fearless...and now....afraid and restricted." He looked despondently at his wheelchair.

"It was so clear," he said pensively.

"What was so clear?" she asked.

"Our reason for being here, our purpose. It's like we're given a mission when we come to this earth, but once here, we forget what it is! A fog goes into our brains and we can't remember."

"What's our purpose?" Georgi asked, intrigued.

Raising himself up onto an elbow again, Andrew said intensely, "To remember who we really are. To know the truth of our birthright and our power. To be that person I was when I was lying on the cloud, filled with the knowledge and wisdom of the ages."

"What *is* our birthright?" Georgi asked.

"To be whole and free. To have the ability and power to overcome every obstacle in our path. Georgi, we were born to overcome all oppression, all illness, all restrictions put on us here." Andrew was getting caught up in the power of the mandate he had been given.

But just as suddenly, the wind left his sails and he dropped back down on the bed. "But now I don't know how," he said morosely.

"I can help you," Doug said from the open doorway.

In response to their startled faces, he said, "I'm sorry for eavesdropping, but Judy sent me to see if you want to come out and sit by the fire with them."

"How can you help me?" Andrew asked. "I want to walk again, but not by sheer physical force. I want to get back to the mental state I was in that allowed my body to be free and work the way it was intended."

"That's what I meant. I can help you get back to that place you experienced, although it goes outside of the medical field."

Piquing Andrew's interest, he urged him to explain, "How can you do that?"

Coming into the room, Doug said, "I practice meditation, and what you experienced is the state we strive to attain. I get glimpses of it every once in a while....and it is bliss!"

"Yes," Andrew sighed.

"And you're right about living it here. They talk in the Bible about heaven on earth and I believe that to be literal, that heaven is a state of mind, not a place. But it's a process, a practice of meditation. As we learn and grow into who we really are, we begin to change the world, as individuals, and then collectively, as more people learn the truth."

"Yes!" Andrew exclaimed, elated in finding a kindred spirit and forgetting his earlier resentment of Doug's presence.

"Some even say," Doug continued, "that the survival of our species depends on us finding out who we are before we self-destruct."

Georgi was looking from one to the other, confused. "But you know who you are," she said to Andrew.

"Oh honey," he tried to explain. "It's so much more than our name or who our parents are. In fact, all that clouds the reality of where we come from, what we're made of, and the vast potential in us."

Doug was nodding his head in agreement. "We've all formed identities that prevent us from living the life we were born to live. Whether it's the identity of a poor or a sick person, we wear that identity like a coat we don't want to take off because we'd feel naked."

"But people don't *want* to be sick or poor!" Georgi said, perplexed.

"No, they don't; they don't want to be a victim either, but circumstances have led them to believe that. Just like you believed Mike and Pat were your parents. You were told that; you believed it. We are what we believe we are."

"C.S. Lewis said that," Georgi said, reflectively. She and her sister, Chris, loved to collect quotes.

"Right," Doug said. "We were all born to be free and to thrive, but our beliefs sabotage us."

Georgi could see he was passionate about this and as excited as Andrew to discover a kindred spirit.

"Don't you see, Georgi," Doug said, "we're *all* told lies about who we are from the minute we're born. We're told we can't do this and we can't do that. This is a very negative world we're born into; yet we come from a totally positive one. Polar opposites; what the church calls good and evil. The positive world says, 'Yes! All things are possible.' This world says, 'No, you can't do that.'

"Are you talking about the benefits of positive thinking?" Georgi asked. "I try to catch myself when I'm thinking something horrible and change it into something positive. But that only lasts about five minutes."

"That's because you can't do it on your own," Doug said. "Look, your brain is a computer. Everything you've heard or learned is programmed into it, it's your default setting. The only way of changing the default is to change your brain; and the only way I've found you can do that is to meditate."

"How does meditation change your brain?" Georgi asked.

"When you meditate, you're plugging your brain into a positive electrical circuit and letting it charge and fill you with positive energy. The positive repels the negative, just like a magnet. Those thoughts that hurt and beat you up, are slowly replaced by more positive and truthful thoughts. Your body follows their instructions to heal and shape itself into who you were meant to be. The Bible calls it the light replacing the darkness."

Blushing a little, he said, "I get excited about this and could go on forever. But I don't want to bore or confuse you."

He was so different from other guys she had met. He was freely opening himself up and sharing what meant the most to him. His honesty made her feel comfortable and she had to smile, showing him he was doing neither.

They were interrupted by Hank and Ali, with Ali announcing, "Mom says we have to go to bed." She snuggled in for a hug from her uncle.

Hank stood apart, contemplative. "Are you ever going to walk again, Uncle Andrew?" he asked.

Andrew, giggling from Ali's butterfly kisses said, "You bet I am, buddy!" and pulled him over for a bear hug.

~ ~ ~ ~

"Tell me again about the heaven you saw," Mae said. She was in her favorite lounge chair, finally settled down and knitting on her latest project. Georgi was perched on the large hearth while a fire crackled beside her; Judy was sitting on the floor, leaning up against the couch between John's sprawled legs; and Andrew was inclined to perfect comfort in the remaining lounger.

Georgi let the warmth of the family and the fire penetrate her body, sighing with contentment.

Andrew was slow to answer Mae's question and no one was in any hurry to break the comfortable silence.

"It was so real," he finally responded, "and so magnificent that I don't have the words to describe it."

"In the Bible, it says that in heaven there will be no tears or the sound of crying." Mae said.

"That's the best way I can describe it too, by what *isn't* there: no worry, no competition, no fear, no fighting. There was a huge table loaded with everything we could possibly need or want and an empty chair for me. I could take whatever I needed. And it wasn't just food, but anything at all, like love or courage or health or faith. I could drink it down just like I'm drinking this glass of wine."

He took a sip and reflected, "Everyone around the table was so happy."

"I'd be happy too if I had anything I wanted laid out in front of me like that!" John said.

Andrew continued on dreamily as if John hadn't spoken. "Instead of words coming out of their mouths, it was a melody. Everyone was singing in complete harmony. No one tone or person was the same; each unique, but each one blended so perfectly with all the others, it seemed as though they were one."

He quit talking, slowly developing a scowl.

"What's the matter, Drew?" Judy asked, concerned. "Are you sad you came back?"

Coming out of his reflection, Andrew looked at her fondly.

"Not sad about coming back to you all, but grieved at the sharp contrast to this world we're living in. I remember looking down on everyone and wondering why so many are suffering and fighting and hurting each other over just the *scraps* that fall off the table, when everything they need is right here. Then I remember that I didn't know it was here either."

Mae had been listening intently, letting her knitting lay idle in her lap. "But you go to church every Sunday, Andrew, and you know darn well that God is everything you need."

"That's true," he said. "But seeing for myself and having direct access is something else entirely! Being able to pick off that table whatever I need. Don't you see? Jesus tried to tell the world about this; that we would have direct access to God through His Spirit and be able to do the things He did, if only we believed."

"I do believe Him!" Mae said adamantly.

"So do I," Andrew reassured her. "But then, why isn't anyone actually *doing* those things? Why isn't anyone able to raise the dead, or walk on water?"

No one had any answers to his rhetorical questions, so he answered them himself. "It's because believing and *knowing* are worlds apart.

"Wow," Judy said. "I never thought of it that way."

Smiling sadly at Georgi, Andrew said, "I know now what it feels like for you to have one foot in this life and one foot in your past life, confused as to where you belong."

"It's like you both have to take the best from both worlds and live in between them," Judy surmised.

Smiling, Andrew said, "There you go again, Sis, being so right and so smart."

"I've been thinking about that," Georgi said reluctantly. "I guess now that you're home and have Doug to help you, I should go back to Cleveland and look for another job.

"You could just as easily look for a job here," Mae piped up.

"You could come work with us at TLC," John suggested.

"You could stay here and go to college," Judy volunteered.

Overwhelmed with emotion, she looked around the room, speechless.

"I have a question for you," Andrew said. "If you had no fears or restrictions and you knew you had an army backing you up in any decision you made, what would you most want to do?"

"That's a really good question!" Judy said. "Now who's the smart one?"

"That really *is* a good question," Georgi said, "but I don't know if I have an answer. I haven't thought about anything other than getting a job so I can pay my bills."

"Well, I'd like you to think about it," Andrew said. "Why don't you sleep on it? Tomorrow's a new day."

~ ~ ~ ~

The house was completely still when Georgi came downstairs the next morning; so different from the pulsing-with-life home she had come to love. But this early stillness had its own ethereal quality, she decided, as she came into the kitchen. The morning light was peeking through the shutters and had escaped its restraints in several places in order to crawl across the counter and illuminate her search for something to eat.

Somebody was up, she realized when she saw that coffee had been made, and poured a cup for herself. She was buttering a bagel when Mae came into the kitchen from the laundry room.

"You had a good sleep," she announced proudly, as if she had everything to do with that. "Can I make you something to eat?"

"No thanks, Mae," Georgi said around a mouthful of food. "Hope you don't mind if I helped myself."

Mae was about to empty the dishwasher, but stopped to look at her. "You don't have to ask for anything, child. You thought any about staying here with us?

"Oh, I've definitely thought about it," Georgi said. "I love it here." Finally realizing that it was much later than she had thought, she asked, "Where is everybody?"

"Andrew and Doug are in Andrew's room doing some physical therapy and everyone else is at work or school."

"I slept through all that?" she asked, amazed.

"You're getting comfortable here," Mae said matter-of-factly. "I'm about to go to the grocery store. You want anything?"

"Some more of those bagels!" Georgi said with a giggle, licking the crumbs from her fingers. "That was delicious. Do you want me to come with you?"

"I've got my own pattern, thanks," Mae said, "but you can go ask Andrew if he wants anything special before I go."

Knocking on Andrew's door, which was ajar, she saw Andrew lying prone on his bed and Doug sitting on the floor beside him. Doug's legs were tucked underneath him in a way that looked extremely uncomfortable. They looked up at her when she hesitantly entered.

"I'm sorry to interrupt," she said, "but Mae wants to know if you want anything at the grocery store."

"Good morning, honey!" Andrew said. "No, I don't want anything, but Doug was just about to show me how to meditate. Do you want to join us?"

"Uh, sure. I'll be right back."

After giving Mae the answer she was waiting for, she came back and shut the door. "Do I have to sit like that?" she asked Doug.

"No," Doug laughed. "You can sit on that straight-backed chair if you like."

Nervously, she asked, "Are you going to hypnotize us?"

"Oh no, nothing like that," Doug said. "You'll be totally aware of your surroundings and your thoughts. The goal is to focus all thought on your breath. But it takes a lot of practice."

"Why is that so hard?" Georgi asked.

"I call it the battle of the brain," Doug answered, "and it's been going on since the Garden of Eden."

"What does the Garden of Eden have to do with this?" Andrew asked.

In explanation, Doug said, "In the Garden of Eden, God told Adam and Eve not to eat from the Tree of Knowledge. I believe that to mean not to worship our brain and all the knowledge we can accumulate. Don't get me wrong, I believe our brain to be one of the most miraculous things we've been given. It is the most complex computer system ever made and to this day, scientists still don't totally understand it. Even the most knowledgeable and intelligent among us use only a small fraction of their brain. We can train our brain to solve extremely complex mathematical equations or to learn ten foreign languages. It is a wonderful thing, our brain, I'm not saying it isn't. What I'm saying is that we allow our brain to be in control."

"But our brain *is* the control center of our body," Georgi said, confused.

"Let me put it this way," Doug said. "If we think of our body as a car, our vehicle while we're here on earth, then our brain is the engine. Everything we ever experience, every bit of knowledge we've gained, every belief we've formed goes into this computer system and is stored. However, these beliefs and opinions carry emotions with them and we let these emotions steer us and make our decisions. As miraculous as it is, we give the brain way too much credit and control. It's our engine, but we're supposed to drive the car. We're not supposed to be the passenger, yet that's what happens when we let the brain be in control. We call it God's will or fate, when in reality, its faulty programming."

"In meditation we basically plug it into the "re-programmer," which changes the default setting and allows you to take over control of the car, the way it was designed. Real freedom is when you can control your thoughts and rise above your emotions so they don't run your life and make your decisions for you. Your mind was created to be your servant, not your master."

"All this talk about training and discipline makes it sound like punishment to me," Andrew said, chuckling.

Doug agreed, "Well, it's not really pleasant sometimes in the beginning, it can be very frustrating. But think of it like exercise. Our brains are muscles too and when we exercise our muscles, it's not always fun. We do it because we want the benefits."

"What exactly is the exercise we're doing?" Georgi asked.

"We're striving to get to a place of total focus," Doug said. "Focus is power. We want to focus all thought on our breath going in and out of our body. It's that focus that helps train and rein in our thoughts. They're like wild horses, running all over the place until we can rein them in and train them to pull our wagon; in this case, our mind. They're supposed to work *for* us, but you'll see just how wild and unruly they are when you begin."

"I get it," Georgi snickered, "my car has horse power!"

Laughing at her joke, Andrew said, "So the focus is to focus."

"Exactly," Doug said. "When another thought comes into your mind, just blow it out of your body with your next exhale. But be patient with yourself when your thoughts start to stray, it happens to everybody."

"I'll talk you through the first part and then you'll take it from there, okay?"

"Okay," they both responded, wiggling around to get comfortable.

"Simple instructions, but hard to do," Doug said. "Just focus all concentration on your breath going in and out of your body."

"Think of opening your heart and letting your breath in. I like to say to myself, 'Yes!' when I'm doing this, because that's what it feels like to me. You may feel like crying or laughing, and that's okay. They'll be happy tears."

~ ~ ~ ~

Sometime later, the bedroom door opened and Mae peeked her head in to ask Andrew if he wanted some lunch.

"Are you all asleep?" she asked, when she saw that everyone had their eyes closed. "How can you all sleep sitting up?" she asked Doug and Georgi.

"No, we're not sleeping," Andrew answered. "Doug is showing us how to meditate."

"Meditate?" she asked, astounded. "That's witchcraft, Andrew! She came full into the room with a hand on each of her stout hips.

"No, no, no," Andrew exclaimed. "It's not witchcraft at all! In fact, quite the opposite."

Doug hastened to add, "We're just clearing our minds to…"

Interrupting him, she said, "An empty mind is the devil's playground, young man." To Andrew, she said, "You're playing with fire, Andrew," then turned and stomped out of the room, leaving the door wide open.

"I've heard that, too," Georgi said timidly. "That it's witchcraft, I mean."

Thinking a minute, Doug explained, "The ancients believed our breath to be God's Spirit in us. People around the world have called it many names, but the Bible says that God breathed his Spirit into us. Think about it: Breathing is the very first and the very last thing you do on this earth."

"So," Andrew said, "when we're focusing on our breath, we're actually connecting with God?"

"Yes!" Doug said. "We humans think that we're here all alone and have to figure everything out for ourselves. We reason and plan and fret. That causes fear, which is ultimately our undoing. If there is a devil, as Mae said, his name is Fear. It has deceived us and kept us all victims of the negativity in this world. Fear has kept people from meditating and finding out the truth for themselves."

Andrew was thoughtful. "I've done a lot of praying," he said, "but I never realized until now how much of it was motivated by fear. I see now that for all the times I've asked God to please help me, that prayer was motivated by the fear that He might not, which is a faulty assumption."

"Right," Doug said. "If we can let go of fear and open our hearts to God's Spirit, we come to really see that God is *for* us and backing us up every step of the way. We don't have to ask. So many times we don't even know the right questions to ask or even what we need. We pray and pray for what we think we need, when all along, the root cause of the problem is something else entirely. If we can rise above our own thoughts and reasoning and hypothesis, and just allow God to show us, we're very often surprised!"

"When we were meditating, I could see the banquet table I saw when I was in a coma," Andrew said, wistfully. "It felt like I was drinking from that table again when I breathed in. What you're saying is that I may not know what item I should choose off the table; that the choosing itself is my form of reasoning, but if I breathe in, what is given to me will be *exactly* what I need."

"Yes!" Doug said. "Going back to the Garden of Eden, meditation is the Tree of Life that we're supposed to eat from. We can have our heaven on earth, but it requires trust and letting go of our own thoughts and beliefs, and hypothesis, which is what the mind fights so desperately to hang on to. Our mind tells us it needs to be in control, yet the irony is that when we realize our real power, we are more in control of our minds and our surroundings and our future than we ever were when we were doing all our own reasoning."

"I didn't feel the power and boldness I felt before," Andrew said, disappointed. "How do I get that back?"

Doug answered him with a question. "When you're asleep, you lose a lot of the inhibitions you have when you're awake, or conscious, right?"

"True," Andrew answered.

"That's why you can dream without restrictions, like dreaming you can fly. In your coma state, you had absolutely no fear, which left you wide open to see who you really are; that you're a part of something so much bigger and greater than anything you can imagine with your mind when you're awake and conscious. Compared to the conscious mind, the unconscious mind is infinitely more vast and powerful. As you practice meditation, you tap into your unconscious mind. The power is cumulative, which means it grows the more you do it."

Georgi had been silent, listening intently to their conversation. "Are you sure it's not witchcraft?" she asked, "Because I saw something really strange."

"What do you mean?" Andrew asked. "What did you see?"

"Well, it was just for a split second, but I saw another woman sitting in my chair – right here where I'm sitting, and I thought to myself, *who is that woman?* She looked vaguely familiar. I guess it could have been me . . . except this woman was so strong and confident looking – she was stunning!"

"You just got a gift!" Doug exclaimed. "You were able to see who you really are underneath all the timidity and fear."

"Are you kidding me?" she asked, amazed. "That was ME? She didn't look anything like me! Do you mean that's who I can become?"

"No, I mean, that's who you *are*," Doug said. "That's who you were born to be. It will take some time to shed the fear, and to let go of the lies you've been told, but you will start seeing the real you shine through as you practice meditation."

"That's how I know this isn't witchcraft," Andrew said, "because of the truth in it. I need to talk to Mae."

"It's really hard for someone who hasn't experienced it to understand," Doug said. "We've been told something all our lives, and believe it with all our heart. Until you see and feel the truth yourself, you can't comprehend. Isn't it ironic that the fear and lies that are drummed into us about meditation are the very things that keep us from experiencing the freedom and truth derived from it?"

"Ironic, or plain old deception?" Andrew asked. "That's how I felt when I woke up; that I had been terribly deceived."

~ ~ ~ ~

Georgi was feeling the electrical tension in the air. Mae set dinner on the table and then announced she was going to her room.

Everyone else made small talk until the children went to do their homework, and then Judy said to Andrew, "You guys really upset Mae today. She told me she's very worried about what you're getting yourselves into."

"She thinks meditation is evil," Andrew said. "But Judy, I can't tell you how right this feels. It's only a fraction of what I felt when I was in a coma, but Doug says that, with practice, it will grow and become stronger."

At the look of skepticism on Judy's face, Georgi added, "And I got a glimpse of the real me! All this time, I've cowered; afraid and meek and ashamed. The real me is nothing like that!"

"What's she like?" Judy asked, amused.

"She looks like she can do *anything*!" Georgi said. "Like no one would ever dare take advantage of her; like she could conquer the world!"

"That doesn't sound like such a bad thing," John said.

"No, I don't believe it is either," Judy said. "But it definitely upset Mae."

"I'll talk to her," Andrew said. "But I think I have a solution."

"What's that?" Judy asked.

"I don't want to wait until 'someday' for my heaven. I need to do a lot of meditating to learn how to live in both worlds, and that's going to require alone time. I don't think that's going to be easy to do here."

Looking at Georgi, he said, "Before I tell you what I have in mind, have you thought about what you would do if you had no fear or restrictions?"

Deciding to just go for it, she said, "I've always wanted to write. I mean, I've written, but only for me. I haven't had the courage to submit anything for publication. Plus, I feel like I've just been rambling. But now I've found my subject....my purpose."

"What's that?" Andrew asked.

"To find the woman who is the real me; and then to help other people struggling with mental and emotional handicaps to become the people they were born to be too. I want to be like you, Judy."

"That's admirable," Doug said.

"It sure is," Judy said proudly.

"Well," Andrew said, "then here is my proposition: How about Georgi, Doug and I go to Florida before the rest of you get there for spring break? We can stay for a few months, or however long it takes. We'll have the time and seclusion to study and meditate. I could give Robert some time off to help Georgi go to Cleveland and close out her apartment and I'll spend that time executing the paperwork necessary to hand over the business to you, John."

"Whoa, wait a minute," John said. "You know I'll take care of things until you get back. You don't have to turn it all over to me now. Let's wait and see how it goes."

"I know you will, John. But I want to get away from it entirely for an indefinite period of time and you need the authority to make decisions and sign whatever needs to be signed. I'll be a phone call away, but TLC is your baby now."

"That's one hell of a vision you have," John said. "I respect it, but I don't have to like it. I didn't have the faith you had in finding Georgi, though, so I will defer to your vision."

Andrew nodded his gratitude to John, then turned to Doug. "I don't even know what your situation is, are you married?"

"No, I'm not married," Doug said. "This is no decision for me at all. I'd love to go with you and put into practice my beliefs that our spiritual, mental and physical components are inseparable. I'm not able to do that in a purely medical capacity. I'd probably have to quit working for the company I'm working for, though."

"That's no problem for me," Andrew said. "I'll pay you independently."

"Wait a minute," Judy broke in. "I'm a little concerned that you're going to try to walk before your body is healed and ready," she said to Andrew, "like in the hospital."

"It sounds like we're saying to face the fear and do it anyway," Doug said. "That's not what we're talking about here."

"Then what are you saying?" Judy asked.

"When I was in the hospital," Andrew explained, "I woke up and I *was* whole, but the fear came back and now I'm not. It's a mindset I'm trying to attain, something totally different than having the fear and doing it anyway. I have to learn how to be whole again."

Doug added, "It's like Georgi saw who she was born to be, but it's going to take time for her to fully realize and incorporate that truth. She's going to have to test it out and grow into her bold, beautiful self," he said, giving Georgi a smile.

Everyone turned to look at her.

"So do you want to come with us?" Andrew asked.

"Yes!" she shouted.

Chapter Twenty

"Thank you so much, Uncle Robbie, for helping me get rid of that old furniture and pack up my apartment."

Georgi and Robert were driving a small U-Haul to Pennsylvania with the things she wanted to keep from her apartment.

"No problem," Robert said. "I'm just happy you're going to live closer to me now."

"You know we're going to Florida, right?"

"You'll be back." Robert took his eyes off the road for a second to smile at her. "I have to tell you that I'm very proud of the way you handled yourself back there."

She had called Jake to tell him that if he wanted his things from her apartment, he should come get them. Just as she and Robert were putting the last few pieces in the truck, Jake arrived, carrying a big chip on his shoulder.

He pulled Georgi off to the side and said to her, "I can't believe you're doing this, Linda. You made promises to me. We made plans for a future together."

With a heavy heart she said, "We were never meant to be together, Jake."

"We used to be good together, until you changed into a stuck up snob," Jake said.

"I didn't change, Jake. You didn't know me. I'm not stuck up, nor am I naïve and gullible and unable to take care of myself. I've seen a lot more of life and living than you know, and just because I was meek and compliant when we met, it doesn't mean I'm ignorant of the ways of men or of this world."

Jake was looking at her dumbfounded, and for the first time since she'd known him, didn't have a retort.

"And by the way," she continued, "did you make those phone calls to Andrew?"

Andrew had confessed to receiving phone calls that he thought had come from Jake, although he wouldn't come out and accuse him and he also wouldn't tell her the terrible things the person on the other end of the line had said.

"I can't believe you would accuse me of something so low, Linda," Jake said belligerently. "You can't be satisfied with breaking my heart, so you have to attack my character too?"

"Funny, you didn't even ask me what phone calls I'm talking about," she said sadly. "And you didn't exactly deny it either."

Stuttering, Jake said, "Of course I deny it, Linda. But they have you so brainwashed, you're not going to believe me."

"No, Jake, I'm not brainwashed by them or by you. No one can tell me what to think or believe."

"Now don't go putting that on me too, Linda! I never tried to brainwash you!"

"Manipulation is just another word for it," Georgi said, "and you can yell all you want, but it doesn't change things. It's all about control, Jake, and I'm the one in control of me."

She said goodbye to him and walked back to her uncle, who had heard the whole conversation.

"I hardly recognized you!" he laughed now. "But seriously, I wish your mom . . . I mean Pat, could have been that strong. Her life was balanced on the whims and conceits of Mike. I think she got to the point where she was too proud to admit she had made a mistake, so she just swallowed his lies and abuse."

"That's sad," Georgi said, "but I see how that happens. I also see that no one respects a person who continuously accepts that kind of treatment." Muttering under her breath, she added, "and we don't respect ourselves, either."

They were silent, listening to a country tune on the truck radio.

After a few minutes, Robert said, "She used to be so sweet before she married Mike. She and I used to lay in the grass and look at the clouds and dream together. She had these romantic dreams of a husband and family, but what girl doesn't, I guess."

"It's hard for me to picture her like that," Georgi said.

"I guess it is," Robert sighed. "Maybe her legacy is to show us the necessity of letting go of anger and hurt and betrayal."

"Easier said than done," Georgi said. "I always saw her as someone proud and defiant. I never realized how alone she must have felt."

She remembered the moment she realized that God was for her, not against her. That shift in perspective changed everything and she knew that was the turning point in her life. She also knew that, had it not been for that change in perception and for Andrew, she could have easily turned out as proud and defiant and alone as Pat had been.

"I'm realizing how important our perspective is," she said to Robert. "How it can change everything. It's almost like we're blind until we can see the truth for what it is. Like Mom thought she was doing the right and honorable thing by sticking by Dad. Or like I thought Jake's love was the best thing that ever happened to me. I can't fault Mom, or even Jake anymore, because I realize I've been driving with a lot of blind spots myself!"

"Wow, you're transforming before my very eyes!" Robert laughed.

Laughing with him, she said, "It's not me doing it, believe me! Doug says it's the gift of sight, and that's what it feels like, that I can see."

"Doug sounds like a smart guy," Robert said, "but you're open to it. That's where you're different from Pat. That's why things are changing for you."

~ ~ ~ ~

"Here you go, one cooler for each car," Mae said, fussing over the packing like a mother hen.

They were putting the last few items in Andrew's car and Georgi's Jeep for the long drive to Florida. Doug would drive Andrew's BMW and Chris was coming along to help Georgi drive her Jeep; then Chris would fly back to Cleveland. Right now, though, she and Chuck were off somewhere saying goodbye to each other for their first week apart since their wedding.

"I'm going to miss you, my Mae," Andrew said fondly. Mae never could stay angry at Andrew, he was her pride and joy. They had discussed their fears and feelings at length and Andrew had finally asked her to judge the practice of meditation by the fruit it produced. "You'll see," he promised her, "this is the prophecy spoken over Georgi all those years ago coming to fruition. You were the one who said that Georgi's birthmark signified God's hand pressing the breath of life into her. Meditation *is* the breath of life. She's becoming a strong woman of God, even though it's not the way you thought it would happen."

He looked around now at the long, sad faces that had gathered around them and said, "I'm going to miss you all."

"Cheer up kids," Judy said to the sullen children at her side. "Spring break is only a month away and then we'll be in Florida with them." She swept Georgi into her arms and squeezed.

"You're about to embark on a new adventure. Are you excited?"

"Wow, excited, nervous, scared, sad, happy," she laughed. "I feel like I'm just beginning my life, is that weird?"

Judy smiled and said, "Not weird in the least. Wonderful, is more the word I would use. Just keep that belief and feeling when the past comes back to haunt you. It will only have the power you give it. Doug is going to show you how to put it in its place."

"Why Judy," Georgi smiled, "it sounds to me like you've done some meditation yourself!"

"I've done research," Judy said smugly.

"What?" she asked in response to Georgi's giggle. "I have an open mind!"

"Oh, Judy. I'm going to miss you so much!"

"I'm a phone call away, always. Now you're going to have Doug to help you," she grinned mischievously.

"Oh stop it," Georgi laughed. "I told you, it's not like that."

Judy laughed with her, admonishing, "Are you feeling undeserving again?"

"I know, I know; I should feel *entitled*!" Georgi laughed.

"Well, whoever you fall for," Judy said, "just don't let anyone stop you from being the bold, beautiful woman you're discovering."

They hugged again and Georgi cried, "I love you Judy."

Robert had been patiently waiting his turn to say goodbye to Georgi and now fake-coughed to get their attention. "It's kind of hard for a fellow to squeeze in between you two," he joked.

Wiping tears and laughing, Georgi turned to give him a hug goodbye. "I've got the best of both worlds with you and Chris and Mary and the whole Lexington crew too!"

"Yep, that's what it's all about," Robert said. "Family isn't always blood relatives."

"Thanks, Uncle Robbie, and congratulations on your promotion!" Robert had been promoted to John's job since John was now officially running TLC.

"Thanks," he said. "Being number two ain't too shabby!" he joked for John's benefit, who had come over to say goodbye to Georgi.

John laughed at the joke but then said seriously to Georgi, "I've got some big shoes to fill, Georgi-girl. I'm counting on you to get Andrew up and running again, and I don't mean physically."

"I'll do my best," Georgi said, giving him a hug goodbye.

Turning to go, John winked and said, "Don't go breaking too many hearts in Florida, darling."

The children were upon her for their turn at goodbye and she saw that Doug was setting Andrew in the car, signifying that it was time to go. She assured Hank and Ali that she would see them in four short weeks and promised to go surfing with them.

Looking around for Chris, she called out to tell her it was time to go.

Mae had been fussing over Andrew until he shut the car door and she then turned to Georgi. "Now, you remember what I told you about what to cook. You two are so thin now, I don't want you wasting away to nothing."

She gave her a hug and said, "Don't worry, Mae. We're going to be so healthy when you see us, you won't even recognize us!"

"There you are," she said to Chris, adding their favored quip: "Chop, chop, lollipop!"

"Don't let her drive too fast," Chuck said, as he hugged Georgi goodbye.

There was a chorus of *bye* and *love you* and *drive safe* and *see you soon!* as they buckled up and started up the road.

Chris began a version of the Jeopardy guessing game they had made up as kids, using their favorite quotes. One person called out the author and the other person had to guess the quote. She now asked: "Henry David Thoreau?"

"Go confidently in the direction of your dreams!" Georgi shouted.

ACKNOWLEDGEMENT AND THANKS:

This book has been an eight year project. I may not have stuck by it without the encouragement and support (and sometime threats☺) of my family and friends. Most especially my son and daughter-in-law, Drew and Toni Long, who have lived with Andrew, Judy, John and Georgi almost as much as I have and have given me more help than I could possibly recount here. My sister, Linda Rader, and my niece, Jennifer Wanchick, have given me support and the encouragement to finish; my friends and editors: Anne Bellissimo; Colleen Bruno; and Janet Quinn were instrumental with their advice and encouragement. I couldn't have done it without all of you and I'm so fortunate to have you in my life! Last but not least, I want to say to all three of my sisters, I love you and always will. No matter where we are on life's path, we share a bond that can never be broken.